YBOR CITY

The Three Kings of Ybor
Volume 3: A Reunion of Beasts

Written By Rock Kitaro

www.StageInTheSky.com

Copyright 2015

**Cover and interior photos provided by Jen Poblete
and Brandy Scaglione of Exposition Photography**

Table of Contents

<u>Recap of "The Three Kings of Ybor: Volume 2:</u>
<u>The Wolves of the Syndicate"</u>

As if the mere mention of his name wasn't already a paralyzing thought, the spectacular destruction caused by Braden Pierce against the Salazar Cartel was sensationalized on almost every evening news station in the Empire. This cast a harrowing light on the Pierce Corporation with many influential figures in the press beginning to sling allegations at the billion-dollar machine with accusations about their involvement in the criminal underworld.

Detective Inspector Angel Gazi is one of the few honest cops who has been actively pursuing Braden for the past two years. But every time he manages to catch a viable lead, it falls under intense scrutiny for its seemingly supernatural circumstances and borders along the lines of investigating a hoax like the Loch Ness Monster. Serving as a private investigator, the mysterious Gavin Hassell offers his assistance in finding enough incriminating evidence to convict Braden once and for all. Weary of Gavin's hidden motives, Det. Gazi reluctantly accepts his help, fully aware that Gavin has the Furyx Gene which gives him and Braden their enhanced senses, strength, speed and dexterity.

And finally, after spending close to four years abroad, a golden haired beauty returns in the form of a 19-year-old Eliza Christie. In her time away she's made the astonishing transformation from a vindictive curse-slurring brat to a mature young adult with her heart set on entering the world-renowned Medici. Or so it seems. By a chance encounter, Eliza meets another freshman who has lost his father in a tragic circumstance quite similar to her own. Robby is a good-natured down-to-earth good-guy who also just so happens to be a Class-A cyber security hacker.

So when he openly reveals a frequent hangout location for one of the syndicate's most lethal assassins it never crossed his mind that Eliza might want to go pay a visit.

Warning: The following volume contains graphic violence and realistic profanity.

Chapter 10 – A Fight in Ybor City

Ybor city was the American Empire's new sin city. While Tampa's top ten percent lingered around downtown Tampa and Davis Island, the rest of the population flocked to their very own version of the Las Vegas strip. It was a heaven for anyone looking to indulge in the seven deadly sins. The booming development market that soared over the past three years made it possible to renovate the old brick cigar buildings and breweries to make room for more venues and larger concert halls.

Massive plasma screens replaced the billboards and posters with mute interchanging commercials. These commercials promoted the hottest trends and brands of the Pierce Corp's subsidiaries. But as you continued to travel to the heart of Ybor, the plasma screen billboards promoted more brow-raising promos of risqué adult toys and the latest innovative sex positions that would make the Karma Sutra seem like a children's book.

The roads were numbered in a grid system, each street competing with the next to drive consumer traffic with the boldest marketing tactics. The most famous of these streets was 7th Avenue West. This was the wide thoroughfare that played host to dozens of annual parades, Expos and licensed vendors setting up shop to show off their inventions. There were always contests going on ranging from dance competitions and car shows to displays of superhuman feats granted by bionic prosthetics and performance enhancers. Creative and ambitious body modifications were celebrated and cheered for as tourists snapped photos of them along the sidewalks. One regular was becoming quite famous for modifying himself so much that he looked like a full-fledged Minotaur.

Every culture known to man walked the streets with pride and an in-your-face air of self-respect. There were six giant arcade pits the size of football fields showcasing the latest virtual arcade games that was very popular with the college crowds. Bragging rights for the trophies and top ranks in the leaderboards were taken very seriously. Soccer fields and basketball courts were created right on the black top of several abandoned overpass bridges with the golden glow of the Halo providing ample light deep into the night.

People traveled in packs and it wasn't unusual to see celebrities and rock stars making an appearance. In some parts of Ybor, if you were walking the streets you wouldn't be able to talk on a cell phone or even someone standing next to you unless you were shouting. A plethora of live music poured out from the near 300 dance clubs, bars, virtual harems and strip clubs.

Gambling and underground street fights at the privately owned casinos brought in millions of dollars every day. While all activities were supposed to be regulated by both local and imperial law enforcement for the amount of tourism it brought in, the locals knew that after midnight everything was run mostly by the sophisticated grip of the Barreira crime family. And Ybor was too big, too popular, with too many alleys and blind spots to simply miss out on the opportunity to cash in on the drug, gun, organ and cyborg prosthetics trades.

After midnight, if you looked like you were worried about getting mugged, raped or jumped, chances are that you'd probably get mugged, raped or jumped. The rumors about the district were true. Every night, someone was murdered in Ybor. In a district where competition was fierce between club owners, rival street racing and motorcycle clubs, brawls and stabbings were almost guaranteed with a clan mentality. That being said, anyone who walked the streets of Ybor after midnight was either experienced enough to handle themselves, or had connections to someone or some faction that could protect them.

One of the more popular spots in Ybor city was an obnoxiously loud spot owned by one of Richard Barreira's son-in-laws, Tito Renaldo. Club Havoc was a massive dance hall, a three-story building that ambitiously combined the haunting Russian architecture of dark colored onion domes at the top of its Gothic stone exterior. Its white strobe lights were controlled by an advanced computer system. The blinding lights, flashy cars, and the sexiest of go-go dancers who worked up a sweat on platforms outside the entrance made the rich and famous gravitate to the club like bees to the honey.

People didn't go to Club Havoc just to drink and socialize. They came to score drugs, get high and maybe "get lucky" right there on the dance floor. It was the epitome of decadence and debauchery that would make the pagan Romans grin. There were rules of course. Mainly a simple rule of respecting house authority. Tito Renaldo's preferred method of execution to set a noose around his victim's neck while they sat in the passenger seat of a car. The car would then speed off with the other end of the rope tied to a fixed structure like a fire hydrant. The force of the pull would nearly pull the head and half of the victim's spine up through the neck. It was a horrible method that struck fear in not only rival gangs, but the police as well. That being said, there was hardly any interference with Tito Renaldo's cash flow.

More go-go dancers worked their seductive magic as they gyrated and shimmied inside of spherical cages that hung in random elevations from the ceiling. The broad dance floor looked like a pulse of ants jumping up and down to the bass heavy urban music as flashing lights waved over them. It was packed with hardly any space between the guy and girl partners and the next couple dancing beside them. Most tourists and foreigners couldn't handle the scene and there have been hundreds of incidents over the year of people passing out. The bouncers weren't hired just to keep the peace, but also to get rid of bodies and accommodate cops who needed their monthly fee.

The 2nd and 3rd floor served as a VIP section that overlooked the stage and dance floor. The elaborate walkways were designed by someone who had a fetish for twisted black painted steel and shiny chains. The walls were made of a thick white frosted glass panels that allowed the exterior swirling white strobe lights to penetrate through. Every dark leather padded booth along the wall was wide enough to sit twelve people and every table. And on this night, every booth was full.

The intimidating party of Braden Pierce, Sean Pierce, Lazar Malenkov and Forrest occupied one of these booth tables. The nineteen-year-old Sean and Forrest were draped in the latest styles money could buy fit for the club atmosphere. Lazar was dressed maturely as his aged dictated, sporting a black designer's suit with a purple vest underneath. And big brother Braden flaunted a more edgy laid-back style, wearing relaxed fit dark jeans, boots, and a white tank top under a stylish brown wholly collared jacket.

Six exclusive high priced escorts were sent to accompany them, compliments from the owner. Seven Black Creek soldiers were posed as bodyguards with sunglasses. They stood away from the table next to the railing with short broadswords concealed under their jackets. The VIPs in the neighboring booths couldn't help but to stare at them with envy, wondering who they were or what they did to attain such service.

Sean and Forest had been knocking backs shots for two and a half hours. The strippers thoroughly enjoyed their company, despite being fingered and molested here and there. Braden remained sober. With his katana propped up against his shoulder at the end of the booth, Braden forced a smile whenever there was a joke said, but mostly stared off into space, gazing at the hypnotic hips of the go-go dancers in cages.

Adele was the stripper who decided to sit next to Braden, a young Colombian woman in her mid-twenties. At a solid six feet, she was almost as tall as Braden with smooth caramel skin, perky double Ds and long legs that accentuated an even muscle tone, probably due to strict regimen of salsa dancing. Seeing all the other ladies at the table having a good time, Adele was beginning to get annoyed with her assignment. Sean noticed and found it all amusing.

"Braden!" Sean shouted from across the table. "Goddamn my nigga! Will you cheer up, already! Shiet man! This is just the vacation we needed."

Lazar and Forrest had been so engrossed with their own entertainment that they hadn't noticed. "Jesus Christ, Braden. What in the bloody hell is wrong with you?" Lazar asked.

Braden grinned as he reached forward and grabbed his glass of vodka and citrus soda. Adele watched with an agitated sneer as he slowly brought it in and drank like a man who had just gotten out of prison and wanted to savor the moment for an eternity. "I'm good, fellas. Don't worry about me." He assured them.

"I ain't complaining. Braden's always been a tight ass. Let the man do wants." Forrest said as he continued massaging a handful of breast.

Sean's sharp vision caught sight of a bodyguard snatching a wine glass off the tray of a sexy waitress that just walked by. He laughed at the sight. "See man! Even our security knows when to taker easy. Right?"

The bodyguard heard Sean speaking about him and took it as a sign of approval, thus allowing him and several others to lower their shoulders a bit. Lazar and Forrest laughed out loud as the other burly bodyguards joined in and raised their glasses to Sean, throwing cheers his way and making him feel popular. Braden smirked, happy that his little brother was enjoying himself. Then he shot the guards a stern look. The bodyguards took the hint and put down their wine glasses.

Annoyed with Braden's sour disposition, Sean removed his arm from around his escort and leaned over the table. The brothers looked each other in the eye, the white strobe lights flaring on and off of them. Even amongst the loud music, the Furyx users could hone in and hear each other clearly. Even if their escorts couldn't.

"Look at him, man. It's like he's not having fun unless he's swinging his fucking sword at somebody's face. This isn't good man. This isn't healthy." Sean barked.

"The little one has a point there, Braden. You're not even twenty-one, yet you carry the look of a man who's lived and fulfilled his entire life. You're still young. Make mistakes. Get into trouble. You'll have plenty of time to regret things when you're older eh? My brother Ulrich told me when he served in the army, you couldn't survive the days without sleep, and bathing and proper shits unless you knew how to laugh." Lazar told him.

Braden nodded, raising his hand to massage his forehead with the index and middle finger. It was freezing outside, but the body heat had raised the interior temperatures to the point that he could feel the humid moisture beneath his fingertips.

"The authorities will approach from every front." Braden warned. "And the old man holsters his most valuable weapon? Why? It's ridiculous. Something's not adding up and it just doesn't feel right. We shouldn't be here."

With a wide taunting smile, Forrest leaned over closer to Braden and Adele. "Braden. Braden." Forest whispered out to him, his breath fuming with alcohol. Adele gave a cute chuckle before batting those long eyelashes at Braden. She began kissing his neck ever so gently.

"Look at this piece right here." Forrest began to sing along with the beat of the music. "See these titties. See these lips. These are all for you. Those lips are just waiting to perform fellatio. She wants to. Cause she wants you."

"I want you. I want you!" Adele whispered.

"Fellatio!" Forrest whispered emphatically before laughing out loud.

"Let me suck your dick." Adele repeated to Braden. She then leaned over and put her arms around him, tenderly kissing his neck and working his way up to his cheeks. Braden wouldn't let her lips touch his. And Sean and Lazar watched dumbfounded at the lack of effect the skinship had on him. They couldn't believe it. It was like watching a documentary on TV, as if Braden wasn't human at all.

Everyone knew the tradition of Club Havoc. From 9p.m. to 2a.m. the DJs would blasts the latest innovative dance and mainstream contemporary songs. But after 2a.m., music in Club Havoc would transition from the dance to grooving heavy metal. And on that particular night, one of the most popular heavy metal bands was in town and had taken the stage. Sean smiled with annoyance as the hip-hop gradually faded out. He could see the band setting up on stage.

"Damn. Whelp! That's our cue. Let's finish this at your deep island penthouse. Shall we ladies?" Sean invited.

Lazar laughed. "Who said you could use my penthouse? Cheeky bastard."

"Whatever Laz, we know you like the company. The flat's too big for you anyway." Forrest joked. The ladies all eagerly agreed as Sean stood up and escorted them out of the booth.

"You coming, lad?" Lazar asked.

Braden was still seated in the booth, his eyes still fixated on the go-go dancers. Sean approached to stand over Braden, gently petting his short wavy hair. "Nah man. You know he likes this garbage."

He handed Adele three hundred dollars. "Stay here and keep him company, will ya babydoll?" Sean told her. Adele flashed a brief smile as she rolled her eyes and snatched the cash.

Sean laughed before leading the convoy of Lazar, Forrest, escorts and three bodyguards down the black stairwell and out of the club. Four bodyguards were ordered to stay behind and protect Braden. The band had just kicked off. A guitar rift was just now picking up in tempo. Braden held a glass of vodka close to his face and stared at the ice cubes. He took in the strong citrus fumes, gradually began bobbing his head to the infectious kick drum.

Adele scooted away from him and lit up a cigarette that she took from her purse. Taking in a puff, she just sat there and observed the way Braden seemed entranced by the music. When the hip-hop and club music was playing, Braden seemed like he was attending a monotonous church sermon. But when the metal began to play, Braden was engaged like a cobra to a snake charmer.

Braden was aware of his condition. He never understood what it was about heavy guitar riffs and rapid-fire kick drum that captivated him. Whatever it was, he knew without doubt that it was one of the pleasures that brought him peace in life. Everyone else were either in the mosh pit having their way with each other, or banging their heads wildly to the beat on along the sides of the dance floor. Braden slowly brought in his glass and drank the last of his vodka before wiping the ice-cold glass across his forehead.

As the band's song kicked up into a full heart-pounding chorus, Braden smiled in a dazed languid expression. It seemed as if his soul had left his body. For however long that outer body experience captivated him, it would end before the beginning of the band's second song. In his daze, someone approaching had caught his attention. At first, he thought he was hallucinating.

Down the walkway, a stunning tall woman showcased a stunning display of Punk Lolita fashion. She wore a Victorian cupcake skirt that was in layers of black and white. Her top was covered by a black see-through mesh of a devilishly sly cat over a white halter-top. Fishnet stockings wrapped up her arms and legs. Each step she took seemed to accentuate the sexy muscle definition in her tight tan skin tone. Her outfit was riddled with a homemade design of buttons and safety pins over random sections. The girl had short black hair and enchanting smoky eyeliner. The skirt of her swaying hips rocked from side to side, shaking its ruffles with a sharp jerk. A gloss of sweat over of her well-defined tan collarbone and neckline glistened in the white strobe light. She was promiscuity personified.

This woman knew what she was doing. With her bold seductive gaze, she aroused almost every producer, rapper and socialite she passed. Her slow procrastinating strut evoked the envy of girlfriends and escorts alike. And while Braden was initially entranced by her supermodel figure and eye-popping visuals, he was beginning to find something unnerving about her. It was inexplicable. His eyes gradually transitioned from a lustful haze to an awareness of danger. The four bodyguards assigned to protect him were caught off guard just like everyone else.

Braden squinted his eyes, involuntarily using his Furyx vision to focus in on her and blocking out the flashing strobe lights. It was by instinct that he noticed she was wearing dark stone-gray contact lenses over naturally green eyes. His heart started to pound. As if he were staring into the eyes of a lioness about to pounce, for the first time in his life, he found himself petrified.

Adele noticed his concern and shouted, "What's wrong with you?"

Braden wasn't hearing her. He simply mumbled under his breath in a tired stretch. "Where have I seen you before?"

The ears of the approaching seductress twitched. Through the explosion of strumming guitars, pounding kick drums and cheering headbangers, the woman had heard Braden's words. She knew she had to act immediately. With a beaming smile of anticipation, the woman reached for something that was strapped along her lower back. Braden watched as she pulled on a strap to reveal a shimmering short bladed katana sword resting in a white ivory sheath that donned a light-green leaf design.

Braden's instincts kicked in. In the blink of an eye, Braden dove out of the booth just as the woman covered ten feet in a single dash. In that single leap, she drew her sword and lunged it into the black leather cushion where Braden's heart was positioned just moments before. Shocked and confused, Braden sat up with his back on the floor, crawling backwards in a crab walk.

With her hand still on the Ivy sword, a disguised Eliza slowly turned to Braden with a squinty-eyed sneer. The two closest bodyguards drew their broadswords and ran for her. Eliza dodged a fast swing aiming for her head and sunk her blade into the man's chest. Whilst shoving the man back by the blade in his chest, Eliza stayed low, pulled her blade out and gave an upward crescent cut to slit the other bodyguard's throat. A sharp line of blood spit Adele in the face. The echoing glass piercing scream that followed stopped the music.

People on the stage and first floor were drawn to the screams. Celebrities in the VIP section were scared out of their minds. Drinks spilled over and heels broke off as everyone shouldered their ways down the walkways and stairs to storm out of the exits.

Braden's last two bodyguards drew their swords and ran for Eliza. These were Black Creek soldiers. The best of the best. It's not like they swung wildly hoping to get a cut at her. They were military trained to be efficient and lethal. Direct and straight for the kill. But just as they leaned back to give their swings momentum, with her Furyx speed she was able to slide in between them and swing her blade from the left to the right. It was a low flat line horizontal cut that severed their kidneys and intestines.

As the bodyguards fell grabbing the side of their bodies, Braden pulled himself together. His stunning disbelief turned to silent rage. Eliza watched as Braden reached for his own long katana and picked himself off the floor with an eerie calm composure. Still wearing an insane wide-eyed look of excitement, she stood up straight and turned her shoulders to face Braden straight on. The muscles in her cheeks twitched anxiously as she raised a hand and yanked off the black wig, releasing the long curly blonde locks.

"You! I know you from somewhere!" Braden growled.

Saying nothing, Eliza simply squinted her eyes, scoffed with the suck of her teeth and shoved the wig towards Braden's face. Braden drew his katana from its black sheath and split the wig into two pieces. Before he could pull his blade back for another move, Eliza was already in his face. Braden had to shift backwards and move quickly to avoid Eliza's graceful blur of well-coordinated swings.

Eliza's new fighting style was that of the ninjitsu Hideo taught her, mixed with the Brazilian capoeira style that she learned from Boa. It looked more like a dance, unpredictable and beautiful. Her feet and athletic toned legs were in constant perpetual motion. She lowered and raised her height without thought, standing up straight and descending into a flattened squat with ease and fluidity. Every time she swung her sword, she did some kind of spin or pivot, moving from the front to the side of her opponent. Thus, Braden was overwhelmed with the lack of space from the booths and balcony railway.

Eliza finally came close enough to knee Braden in the stomach. With Braden hunched over in throbbing pain, Eliza palmed his neck to lift him up. He let out a loud gargling grunt as she shoved him back with surprising strength. Before Braden could regain control, Eliza leaped forward, spun in midair and stomped the heel her left boot into Braden's chest. The force of the attack caused Braden to fly backwards and hit the brick wall at the end of the walkway before bouncing off to fall forward on his knees.

With the air knocked out of him, Braden wheezed to breathe. The frustration in his eyes could not be contained as his fierce gaze gradually lifted from the black metal floor up to Eliza. It was the first time in a long time that he's had his ass handed to him and he didn't like it. Eliza's confidence was growing but she didn't let accomplishment or satisfaction sink in. Tightening her grip, Eliza rushed forward and coiled her arm back for a powerful lunging attack. Just when the tip of her blade came to within inches of Braden's face, a nervous jolt coursed through every nerve in her body. Braden gave a lightning fast upward swing to deflect Eliza's blade. The power and speed behind his sword had completely caught her off guard. While it was the first time Eliza's fought with another Furyx user, Braden had more than his fair share of experience.

As Eliza stepped back in an attempt to rethink her strategy, Braden stepped forward with two hands on his hilt and delivered a hellacious home run swing aimed at her sternum. Eliza was able to turn her shoulders and lift her sword just in time to block his sword edge first, but the force and strength behind his swing sent the blunt side of Ivy driving back into her right clavicle. With her feet not firmly planted on the ground, the strength of his Furyx induced strike sent her entire body flying back through the thick frosted glass panels.

Eliza's jaws rattled and her shoulder blades throbbed as she fell to a scraping halt twelve feet across the rooftop of an adjacent building attached to the club. Pedestrians on the congested streets nearby had heard the high-pitched impact and were curious to know what had happened. They were only able to catch a glimpse of Braden climbing out of the glass hole like a bird of prey swooping down for the kill. It only took but one person to shout, "what the fuck wuzzat!" for a mass of half drunken club-hoppers to rush the club and head up toward the VIP section.

Shaking the shards of glass from her hair, Eliza rolled to a defiant stand. A strap was cut on her now stretched out halter top, bearing her black satin bra. The numbness in her right arm was beginning to wear off, but it never distracted her in the first place. Insulted by her resilience, Braden rushed forward. Eliza managed to block two more arm rattling swings before she covered fifteen feet in an acrobatic back flip to create distance. With Club Havoc packed and over capacitated, people began breaking down doors and pouring into other neighboring clubs and apartment buildings to find out what was happening. Some even began taking out their cell phones to record it.

The metal band in Club Havoc started playing again. As the up-tempo guitar driven soundtrack kicked off, Braden and Eliza stood in their respective stances, glaring as they aimed the tips of their swords at each other.

Braden still could not figure out where he had seen her. "Miss!" He shouted. "I don't know who you think I am, but you're definitely going about this the wrong way."

Eliza whipped a large wad of spit on the grey cement roof. The white strobe lights flashed on and off of her face as she showcased signature squinty-eyed glare. "Get over yourself, ass-douche. Let's see how many dates you can get with your dick cut off." She snarled.

Perhaps realizing that they weren't going to get anywhere with mere words, Eliza and Braden calmly walked towards each other whilst boldly lowering the tips of their swords. Just as they came three feet within each other, the aggressive sword fight began again. Eliza stayed low, using the agility and incredible footwork of a lightweight gymnast to try and avoid each and every one of Braden's nerve-wrecking swings without making metal on metal contact. She also displayed a reckless yet effective skill of switching sword hands in the middle of an attack. With her left hand she'd deliver a swift diagonal swing upward toward Braden's neck. If Braden dodged the swing and her sword went past his neck, she'd let go of the sword in midair and spin around to the side of Braden to catch it with her right hand just in time to block Braden's next move. All of this happened with the fast paced swiftness of a fox and a mongoose in perpetual motion.

A young Italian tourist who had managed to crawl onto the roof from Club Havoc was filming the fight intensely. His shot was focused on the blond girl holding her own against the darker more aggressive male.

"Holy crap. This girl is good. Who are these people?" He whispered with a toothy smile.

While Eliza's moves seemed erratic and acrobatic, basically all over the place, Braden timed his attacks well and hardly ever did anything that wasn't necessary. His swings were lightning fast, powerful and always showed a streak from whence the strobe lights glistened of the expensive steel. Like Eliza, Braden was very agile, never staying in one place for long. He used a relentless method of staying close to her, wearing her down with physical attacks like an elbow to the face or knee to the abdomen while showing impressive wrist work to turn his sword up or down without even swinging it. It was a mental prowess of already having his moves lined up in his head before executing them. No one on earth had such skill at his level.

After a brief performance, Braden and Eliza locked swords. Ignoring her gender, Braden viciously elbowed Eliza twice in the face. As Eliza stumbled back, Braden planted another foot forward and delivered another double-grasped baseball swing. Eliza blocked it, but the force of his blow knocked her chest first onto the pavement with the green leaved Ivy twirling away from her toward the roof gutter.

Everyone was cheering wildly and applauding the performance, none of them grasping the danger she was in. Eliza was beside herself with spite and disappointment. She couldn't believe it. For a moment, she wondered if all of her training and preparation was for naught.

Braden walked to stand over her and aimed the tip of his long samurai katana to point directly between her eyes. Still annoyed with her ever-defiant attitude, Braden calmly asked her. "Who are you?"

Huffing and puffing, Eliza palmed the ground to sit up and shouted at the top of her lungs. "Go the hell!"

Everyone heard and cheered her answer. Braden heard the laughter and understandably felt that it was at his expense. There were people sitting halfway out of window ledges watching the fight. Everyone was staring at him. Laughing at him. Taunting him. But it wasn't their mockery that disturbed him. He knew there was video being recorded. He had let himself get carried away and sooner or later the higher ups were going to find out. And he looked around considering this, Braden failed to notice that Eliza was reaching for razor sharp shuriken contained in a leather patch behind her skirt.

Suddenly, Braden caught a glimpse of a shadowy figure floating closer behind him. Impulsively, Braden quickly raised his sword for a lightning fast backhanded swing followed by another horizontal cut. The shadowy figure used a long double-edged claymore sword to block the two strikes before displaying an amazing ability to leap fifteen backwards and land as soft as a cat on the ledge of the roof. A gasp and an inspired smile formed on Eliza's face as she immediately recognized the beautiful dark angel in the stylish grey overcoat. Gavin Hassell had joined the fight.

Braden's annoyance amplified and the humiliation of being mocked was finally starting to kick in. "All right, now what the hell do you want?" Braden shouted to Gavin.

Gavin grinned as he femininely pulled his long black bangs back into a ponytail. "That girl belongs to me... Braden Pierce."

Braden's heart stopped with shock as he heard his name being mentioned. The sight of Gavin's overcoat blowing in the wind with his long hair jogged Braden's memory. He had no doubts that this was the same man who had been following him for the past few months. Braden was beside himself with rage but hid it well. The most he expressed with a snarling scoff before taking off in a full sprint for the stranger.

Gavin ran along the roof's narrow ledge before launching himself to clear over forty feet in a single jump across the street to another rooftop. People standing on the street watched with amazement as Braden easily leaped above them in pursuit. A round of vocal awes and whoa flowed through the atmosphere as many were beginning to wonder if they were high. What they just witnessed was impossible by normal physics, and yet it just happened. Two men just jumped across the street as if they were squirrels leaping within branches. And it was recorded by hundreds of cameras.

The new paved rooftop was surrounded by red neon lights and the insignia of Tampa's professional football team. Standing across from Braden, Gavin turned and looked up at the huge neon light signs as if Braden wasn't even there. Braden knew he was being toyed with and didn't like it. Not from the likes of some arrogant bastard he never even met.

Gavin's ploy worked. An infuriated Braden ran for Gavin and delivered a swift vertical strike. Gavin easily shifted left to evade the swing and Braden's blade hit the tubes of neon lights. There was an echoing pop along with a spray of sparks that flew out at him stinging his eyes. With Braden half blinded, Gavin confidently stepped forward, wielding his sword with both hands and advanced with a series of strikes.

Unlike Eliza and Braden, Gavin didn't show off lot of fancy steps and jumps, but more so put all of his power and strength into each swing as he was trained in the Marines to do. While one swing would usually by enough to sever a man in two by the hips, Gavin knew Braden had the Furyx. And more than that, he acknowledged and respected Braden's talent as an executioner. Thus, Gavin used the strategy of shifting back and forth six feet at a time with swift speed to attack and evade in a hit and run like fashion, draining his opponents to either chase him or back away.

Braden was faster, but Gavin was slightly stronger and more cunning, using his surrounding to his advantage. It didn't take long for Braden to catch on to Gavin's hit and run scheme and the fact that he was being toyed with pissed him off further. Braden rushed forward and delivered two more horizontal swings aimed for the midsection. Gavin shifted back to evade both of them before leaping higher than that of a basketball goal to land light like a bird atop of the red neon lights sign.

Gavin seemed to be enjoying himself, a stark contrast from his usual apathetic martyred demeanor. He wore a smug look, satisfied with his own strength and the belief that he was indeed superior to Braden.

"Braden! You really shouldn't do things that are bad for your health."

Braden's jaw clinched at the sound of Gavin's voice. God knows that at that exact moment, Braden would've gladly burned down the whole building if time permitted him.

A patrol chopper suddenly appeared as if it had been there the whole time but just hiding behind another building. It shined a spotlight on the rooftop, mainly on Gavin who was standing with valor on the highest point. Gavin eagerly looked up to the light, embracing it with a smile as he ran his fingers through his long bangs that waved with the gust. Turning back to look at Braden, Gavin was disappointed to see that he was nowhere to be found. Braden had darted off the moment the chopper turned on the spotlight. Gavin noticed that everyone watching was applauding his performance as the victor. He then looked across the street. Eliza leaned over with one knee over the ledge. Her arms were crossed and she wore a smirk of admiration. Gavin responded with a gentle smile of his own.

…

Déjà vu and surreal. It was all like reliving a fantastic dream. So reminiscent of that cold night four years earlier, she was once again following Gavin down the sidewalk toward his home. Only this time, she was almost as tall as he was. She didn't stare with admiration like before, but more so walked on an equal footing, disregarding her ruined dark costume.

In College Hills just a few miles north of Ybor district, his apartment was on the top floor of the four-story brick tenement just the same as before. His place had a few minor upgrades however, such as the desk with a computer. But more so it was surprised that he had an entire wall was dedicated to the organizational structure and known affiliates of the Tampa gangs.

Eliza studied the wall as Gavin went through his usual routine of taking off his jacket and shirt and washing his face in the sink. Amongst the maps, documents, and profiles of various associations, the wall showed photos of Braden from the last two years. It was everything any prosecutor would need to put Braden away for life. Eliza couldn't believe it. It seemed he was almost as obsessed as she was to get rid of him.

But she didn't understand Gavin's connection to Braden. From Braden's expression from the fight earlier, it seemed as if Braden didn't even know who Gavin was. If Gavin was following and gathering evidence on Braden for years, why didn't he make himself known? There was also something else. There weren't any photos of Braden in the heat of battle, but nonchalant photos of Braden at a coffee shop or in some club. And in every photo, Braden wore the same gloomy facial expression as if he was deep in thought. The photos of Braden angered Eliza. And then something else struck her nerve that was just the worst. During their fight, Braden didn't even recognize her.

"Why don't you check out the roof?" Gavin suggested.

His sudden husky voice caught her off guard. She turned to see a shirtless Gavin watching her from the sink with the water still running.

"Do you want me to leave the room?" Eliza said with a smirk.

Gavin nodded. "The sun is about to come up. I'll bring you some hot cocoa."

Eliza rolled her eyes with a grin as she picked up her green overcoat hoodie. "Hot chocolate. Oh boy." She muttered as she exited the room.

Gavin stood in the same place by the sink and listened to her footsteps as they walked down the hallway toward for the roof access door. It wasn't until he heard her open the door and start to head up that he stopped listening. He then walked over to his wall of Pierce photos and quickly scanned over everything to see if anything was missing. He noticed a photo of Braden from two years ago was tilted slightly two degrees to the left. Gavin straightened it out back to the way he had it.

On the roof, Eliza sat on the flat cement grainy ledge whilst bundled in her overcoat. There were several heated cages of pet Rottweilers sleeping along one side of the roof. On another side, rows of potted marigolds that could withstand the frigid conditions were in full bloom. Eliza looked toward the east. The cloudy skies were turning a deep indigo from the rising sun that was beginning its ascension. The streets below glowed from the headlights of streaking cars, employees hurrying to avoid the rush hour even though it was a Saturday. It was a serene scene, serenaded with the sounds of the rail transit that sped along the golden glowing Halo overpass nearby.

Eliza showed an uneasy smile of sad nostalgia for her city. She lifted her fish-net covered legs to bring them in close and cover them with the coat. Her breath was visible in the brisk morning air. Gavin approached wearing a thick white sweater and dark blue jeans. His long black hair was pulled together almost in a ponytail and draped over his left shoulder. Eliza giggled at the memory of contrast from his attire before.

"Thank you." She said ever so softly as she accepted Gavin's warm mug of hot cocoa.

Gavin lit up a cigarette and joined Eliza in looking out toward the horizon. "Where have you been?" He asked her.

"Why? Were you looking for me? Did you miss me?" Eliza asked with a smirk.

Gavin scoffed with a grin. "This is the second time I've had to come to your rescue, sunkiss. I see you still have that death wish hanging over your head."

"Trust me. I didn't need it. Don't get me wrong I appreciated the gesture. Good chivalry in all. But I could've taken him out." Eliza took out her small razor sharp ninja stars and showed them to Gavin.

Gavin stood with a look of perplexed expression before letting out a slight chuckle. "Eliza, who the hell do you think you are?"

Eliza laughed haughtily at the question before Gavin became sullen and asked her again in a deeper tone. "Seriously. What the hell did you think you were doing?"

His line of questioning insulted Eliza but she didn't display that patented attitude. She calmly put down the coffee mug and gazed sternly into his clear deep blue eyes. "Alright Gavin, I think you need to get it through your head that I'm not that same little girl throwing herself at you. I've come a long way."

She started to turn her head and stare back out toward the horizon, before she whipped her gaze back to Gavin again. "And I could ask you the same thing. Why were you at that club tonight? And why do you have a goddamn wall dedicated to the Pierce? Starting some kind of fan club, are we?"

Gavin took a puff from his cigarette. "I'm a private investigator. It's my business to know what the little shit stain is up to." Gavin answered.

The two became silent whilst glaring at the horizon, festering at the thought of the Pierce. After a while, Eliza slowly turned to examine the blue eyed angel. Like her, Gavin wasn't the same as before either. There was a light in his eyes. He seemed more alive, with a sense of purpose. In a sense, she wanted to believe that the two of them shared a common goal but there were too many unknowns about Gavin. Other than her own experience with him, she had no idea who he was, what he's done or what he's been through.

"You know…" Eliza started, getting Gavin's attention. "It isn't just him, I'm after. He didn't just wake up one morning and thought, hey, I think I'm gonna kill me a cop today. No. Braden is just a mad dog. It's not just him I want. But all the other dogs like him and the mad men holding their leashes."

Gavin wore a perplexed expression. "The syndicate? You want to take down the whole syndicate?"

As Eliza nodded like it was no huge feat but a mere chore that she had decided to undertake, Gavin walked closer and sat on the ledge beside her.

"Look at me. Eliza, look at me." He told her.

Flattered, Eliza held back her smile as she turned to look into his dreamy dark-blue eyes.

"You need to slow down, alright. Braden…that's one thing. But taking on the whole syndicate is likened to declaring you're going to bring down an entire branch of the government. Damn near every politician, every general, ever mayor and every criminal has ties to the Pierce. Eliza…this is the talk of foolishness." Gavin told her.

Eliza exhaled deeply as she reached over and caressed Gavin's cheek. It was a bold move. Perhaps an intention to show she was no longer just a meager fan.

"Gavin…I believe you're saying that just because you don't think that you could do it. I never asked for this deep twisted sense of malice and malevolence. But I acknowledge that it's there. And while it may seem like I'm alone. I'm not. This world. This city. It's full of sons, daughters, wives and husbands. All of them left behind when their loved ones were stripped away by the sword of the corruption. I'm going to lead those survivors, Gavin. I'm an indivisualist. The phrase, 'that's just the way it is,' won't fly anymore. Because I won't stand for it."

Gavin and Eliza turned east and could just now see the dull blurry outline of the sun fading through the blue clouds that cast a dark blue tint upon the city. It was a scene of yellow city lights under a blue blanket of cottony sky. Gavin took in the last breath of the cigarette before putting it out on the ledge.

"Well…" Gavin said, realizing there was nothing he could do to sway her. "If you ever need any help. Just ask."

Chapter 11 – The 18th's First Member

A constant drumroll of heavy rain fell hard on the roof of Gazi's townhouse. At around 10:30 in the morning, Eliza gradually woke up in her bed after her usual four to five hours of sleep. Despite his crazy schedule, Gazi had found the time to set up the guest room for her, making her bed and putting up the same drapes that were in the room from back when she was fifteen. Lying on her back in the cool dimly lit room, Eliza looked up to the ceiling and stared off into space. She thought of Gavin's blue eyes and the next time she'd be able to see them.

Suddenly she noticed her door that was half-opened, opening up wider. She sat up and smiled as Max strutted into the room and ate some food from out of a bowl in the corner of the room.

"Yeah, that's not gonna stay there for long." Eliza said. And as if the dog understood, Max turned around and looked at her with a whimper.

"No sir! Not in this room! No, no no!" Eliza mocked in a cute high-pitched voice. Throwing the sheets off, Eliza whipped her well-toned legs out of bed.

...

The 706 Kennedy Street Tampa Metropolitan Police Department was one of the largest municipal police forces in the world. It was an eighteen-story complex with two floors underground and it took up most of the Channelside block in the heart of downtown Tampa. It was positioned along the Ybor Channel with quick access to nearly every bridge and main highways to supply reinforcements to any of the remote districts like St. Petersburg, Clearwater, Bradenton and Pinellas Park.

Inspector Detective Gazi's office was on the 3rd floor. Every Inspector of the homicide division had their own office along the 3rd floor walkway that overlooked the 2nd floor bullpen of plain-clothes detectives and sergeants. Outside of every inspector's office sat their assigned assistant's desk, filtering incoming e-mails and addressing phone calls.

Gazi's office was furnished well with a European white and brown couch set and wide windows that overlooked the transport ships stationed in the channel. A constant drone of raindrops pounded against that window as he sat at his desk reading the newspaper from an electronic tablet. His colleagues sat on the other side of his desk, both of them drinking warm coffee as they waited for Gazi to finish. Detective Inspectors Di Mare and Walsh worked in the Criminal Enterprise Division. Being that most of Gazi's homicide cases were related in some way to organized crime, it's understandable how they've come to trust each other over the years as good and honest cops.

"So the rumors are true, eh?" Walsh said in a thick husky accent. Gazi shook his head in disbelief as he turned off the tablet and twirled it onto a stack of reports on his desk.

"I don't believe it. All this time, I thought Braden Pierce was one of a kind. Seems there's more of em." Gazi said in disappointed astonishment.

"Two guys... According to witnesses and bloggers and the talking heads of nearly every godforsaken evening news show. Two men leaped over an entire four-lane intersection to reach the building across the street. Am I the only one thinking we're living in a goddamn science fiction movie here?" Di Mare asked them.

"You were right all along. We need to look into this Furyx Gene, Gazi. The world needs to know that we have these super criminals out there. Over the past few years, LOD casualties have sky-rocketed. This whole time, we've been blaming the training, the equipment or lobbying for the emancipation of those ridiculous gun laws. But now we know why. Let's face it gentlemen. We're not equipped to handle this." Walsh said.

There was a brief moment of silence. The elderly Inspector Walsh's words were hard to swallow given the many decades of service each man had dedicated to the idea of upholding the law piously. There was a knock on the door. Everyone ignored it. Being that it was Gazi's office, he couldn't afford to ignore the persistence as the knocking continued.

"Yes?" He called out.

Gazi's young assistant was a woman named Ashley Rivera. She was a grad student at the Central Tampa, studying for her masters in forensic psychology. With her overly attractive appearance and huge breast that seemed disproportionate to her short Latino figure, she was a constant target of unsolicited attention and sexual harassment. Fortunately for everyone else, she understood and accepted that her beauty was a gift and a curse and simply felt pity on those longing for what they could never have.

Ashley stuck her head into the doorway and was slightly taken aback by the emotionless gaze each inspector wore. "A girl claiming to be your daughter is here? She says she brought you lunch. She's blonde? With green eyes? Says she's your daughter?"

"Yes thank you Ashley." Gazi said sharply to shut her up.

Ashley smirked before exiting from view. Walsh and Di Mare turned to Gazi with a slightly comical puzzled expression. Gazi laughed off the embarrassment as he stood up from his desk and walked toward the door. "It's not like that, fellas."

"Sure Gazi. Sure." Di Mare scoffed.

"You did sleep with that one reporter. Hausermann was her name, right? Remember her?" Walsh brought up, igniting laughter from Di Mare.

Gazi entered the hallway and stood beside Ashley's desk to see Eliza standing with a small cooler in hand. Gazi smiled. "Eliza, do you ever take off that coat?"

"Do you ever look beyond the rack?" Eliza said as she walked past Ashley, subtly throwing a glance at her voluptuous figure.

"I brought you lunch!" Eliza said in a cheerful tone as she walked past him to enter the room uninvited.

"Yes. I see that." Gazi said abruptly. He then turned to his assistant and whispered an apology for Eliza's remark.

"Jajaja!" Ashley scoffed light-heartedly before pushing Gazi in the room and closing the door on him.

"Gentlemen. You might not recognize her but this is Elizabeth. Emil's daughter." Gazi introduced as he walked around to his desk.

Realizing the significance of her background, Walsh and Di Mare stood up with mild astonishment to extend their hands. "I remember your father well, Ms. Elizabeth. He was a good friend. You have no idea how deeply his loss impact the entirety of the force." Walsh told her.

"I remember you." Di Mare said. "You were the little one always butting into our conversations at those get-togethers HR used to set up. You remember don't you, Walsh?"

"Oh yes! Hahahaha! You and Gazi were always going at it. The great Gazi unsaddled by a toddler. Those were monumentous!" Walsh laughed.

"That's because she always thought she was right." Gazi added.

"I was right." She snapped back with a smile.

After the laughter and introduction pleasantries died down, there was an awkward pause. Eliza stood in place carrying the cooler by the handles with both hands. Her raised eyebrows and the gentle press of the lips was a universal gesture indicating that she wanted them to leave. She honestly didn't remember any of them and with the lack of progress on the rising crime wave, it's not like she had any reason to admire them, regardless of her father's relations to them.

"What time is it?" Di Mare asked way too conspicuously.

On the wall behind Gazi, there was a copper clock designed like a sun with rays coming out of it. Everyone awkwardly turned to look at the clock as if they suddenly heard the clock whispering their names.

"Oh. One thirty! Weren't we supposed to meet with Lobos?" Di Mare asked Walsh.

"That's right. Damn plainclothes think breaking the law is part of their goddamn job description." Walsh grunted.

Eliza watched as Walsh and Di Mare nodded their heads and exited the room. Gazi sat with his head propped up in his hand, gazing at Eliza as if to say, "What is it?" Embracing the music of endless rain patter, Eliza simply smiled as she approached and placed the cooler on his glass desk. Then she sat down in one of the two chairs station in front of the desk and crossed her jean-covered legs in normal sophisticated fashion, still wearing her hooded green overcoat.

"Interesting characters you have there." Eliza noted with doubt.

Gazi's eyebrows furrowed. "Eliza, you don't even know them."

"How long has your secretary been working for you?" She asked.

"Assistant. And Ms. Rivera is actually in grad school. You should make friends with her. She could get you into some proper extracurricular activity or sorority or something."

"Do I look like the sorority type?"

"Maybe not the personality, but you certainly look the type." Gazi said with a grin.

"What? Blond and stupid?" Eliza asked.

"No. Blond with an attitude." Gazi said, still wearing a nonchalant grin.

Eliza sighed she casually tapped two of her fingers on her knee. "I brought you lunch."

"Poison?"

"Open the lid."

"Ah. Bomb then."

"Yes Gazi. It's a bomb. Still sharp as a tack, I see."

Gazi and Eliza laughed before she stood up and opened it for him. The cooler contained bags of potato chips, two turkey club sandwiches that she had bought from a gas station and two bottled sodas. She laid it out on the desk before him.

"Eliza, you didn't have to do this." Gazi laughed, deeply grateful.

"Yeah, well! You know…" Eliza said pleasantly.

As she laid the sandwich down on her desk, she caught sight of a thick manila folder. On the corner tab, it had Gavin Hassell's name on it. Gazi noticed her fascination to it as she stood motionless with a near death grip on his sandwich.

"Elizabeth. What is it?" Gazi asked.

Eliza blinked out of her trance and quickly pulled herself together. "Oh yeah. I'm just um…Gazi, how do you know this man?" Eliza asked as she picked up the folder.

With his sandwich halfway unwrapped, Gazi reached over and grabbed the folder from her. He flipped through the pages of photos and reports before giving Eliza a stern look.

"How do *you* know this man?" He questioned.

Eliza's eyes wandered as she fidgeted with a strand of her blonde hair. Gazi casually leaned back in his rolling chair and opened a bag of chips as he watched Eliza suddenly get up and walk toward the windows. Her Furyx vision involuntarily zoomed in on a single raindrop on the window. She could see the tiny air bubbles swirling as the drop slowly trickled down the glass. Then, she turned back at Gazi. She found his cavalier attitude both charming and slightly annoying.

Eliza flattened her back against the cool glass window, her bottom slightly resting on the edge of the ledge. She sighed and began.

"Gazi. You remember that night? The night before you shipped me off for Korea?"

"You mean the night you had me up worried till daybreak? Yes. How could I forget?" Gazi said before taking a big bite out of the sandwich.

Eliza rolled her eyes. "I'm trying to be serious here."

Gazi nodded as he wiped some mayo from the corner of his lips. "Continue."

"Well that night, I was down in Ybor. Some bikers were going to rape me."

Gazi's eyes widened by her revelations but her slight rise of the hand calmed him. "Gavin saved me." She told him.

Gazi released a heavy sigh as he tossed the sandwich on his desk and shook his head. "Elizabeth…"

"I know. I know. I was completely reckless and stupid. But in more ways than one, I wouldn't be here if it wasn't for him." Eliza said with watery eyes.

Gazi got up and walked over to embrace Eliza with a hug. Eliza sniffed with her face planted in Gazi's starch ironed shirt. Gazi tilted her chin up to look into her eyes. "Elizabeth. I'm so sorry."

In a slightly awkward, suppressed fashion, Eliza pulled away from him and wiped her tears as she headed for the cooler on the desk. "Don't worry about it. Like I said. Gavin was there to save me."

Gazi watched as she unwrapped a turkey club. He wondered if she blamed him for not being there for her. "Well next time I see Gavin, I'll have to extend my gratitude." Gazi said.

He walked back over to his desk and sat down. While he appreciated Eliza's honesty, his former feelings of disappointment in the way she used to be were beginning to surface. The two just sat and ate their lunch in complete silence for the next fifteen minutes. Fifteen long, awkward minutes of nothing but rushed footsteps outside the door and rain on the window panels.

"How do you know Gavin?" Eliza asked once again, breaking the silence.

Gazi sighed. He didn't want to tell her, but felt it would be unfair to fail in rewarding her revelations. "He's a private investigator. He sometimes pulls special assignments for me. He's dependable, but... Yes, he's dependable."

"But?" Eliza asked. "Follow through, Gazi."

"But nothing. He's dependable. Like I stated. What else do you want to know about him?"

"Where's he from? What's his background?" Eliza stressed.

Gazi sighed as he opened Gavin's folder and tore off of a page attached to the front flap. He then put it on his desk and slid it over. Eliza began to pick up on Gazi's attitude and detested it as such. Thus, she impulsively leaned over and snatched it off the desk as if it were laid upon a mousetrap. After a quick scan of the profile, she was surprised to see Gazi knew so much about him.

"He's from San Antonio, Texas?" Eliza said in astonishment. Gazi confirmed by nodding his head and gazing at her with a look of skepticism.

Eliza continued to read. "He dropped out of high school in his junior year even though he was in the top of his class. He joined the Marines, even though there wasn't any major conflict. Three years ago, he posted his number on a website after he got his class-cc license for private investigating. It says here that he's worked for some high profile clients, racking in close to a quarter million dollars last year."

It was all very puzzling and didn't make sense to her. He was relatively wealthy yet still lived like a middle to lower class citizen. "How can you afford him?" She asked.

"I can't. The jobs he does for me, he does for free. I don't know why, but he's always there when it comes to scandal that has the breath of Pierce upon it. I like the kid. But his motives are an enigma. I can't help but distrust him. He always says, and I quote, everything I do is for a reason, even if it makes sense only to me." Gazi told her.

Eliza nodded. She understood where Gazi was coming from. Thinking back, nothing Gavin has ever done when it came to helping her made sense. Or rather, it wasn't something any normal person would do.

A cell phone started to ring. It was Eliza's. She reached into her black handbag to pull it out and saw that it was Robby. "Oh cool. He's right on time. He's a good boy." Eliza said with a smile as she put Gavin's profile back on the desk.

"Who's he?" Gazi asked.

"Robby." Eliza said bluntly. "A guy I met at school yesterday."

"After one day? When am I gonna get to meet him." Gazi asked as he watched her gather her things.

"Hopefully never, dick. Why don't you go play with your secretary? She looks like she needs some attention." Eliza scoffed before grabbing her purse and heading for the door.

"Eliza!" Gazi called out.

It was too late. Eliza was already out the door and power walking down the hall.

...

There was still a light rain in progress with a heavy grey sheet shrouding the sunlight. But it seemed to have no effect on the diverse collection of citizens that loitered around the main entrance of the precinct. They were either sitting on benches or standing around a ten foot bronze statue of Lady Justice carrying weight scales in the center of the plaza. Law enforcement personnel were coming to and from. Detainees who were just released or the family members waiting for them to be released covered the walkways.

Heated and annoyed with Gazi's cynicism, Eliza exited the building with an umbrella and powerwalked down the cement steps. She continued until she stood at the end of a platform overlooking a busy intersection and scanned the vehicle windshields for any sign of Robby.

Just then, there was a dull booming explosion that sounded almost like thunder. The people stopped in place with questionable expressions, puzzled, wondering what had happened. The screams that followed, however, indicated that the explosion wasn't natural. Like a herd of livestock being corralled, a wave of dark blue uniforms took off on foot in the direction of the explosion.

Eliza stood in place with her hands tightly clasping on the rail. She pressed on her lips and suppressed her rage to hide a squinty-eyed snarl that she wanted to release. Unlike everyone else, she heard the explosion as if it occurred right in front of her. She identified the sound of twisting heavy metal. The sound of shattering glass impacts from bodies being slammed into building panels. A bomb had just gone off and it wasn't a stretch to assume it had something to do with the ongoing Rosetti-Gacha conflict. Only Kelly Rosetti's men would do something so bold as to set off a car bomb a few blocks from police central. Especially if it meant casualties for Mariana Gacha's family.

"Hey!"

Eliza's blonde hair whipped as she turned around to see Robby standing there in a thick yellow and grey padded coat, carrying an umbrella and his ever trusty faded red baseball cap.

Eliza squinted her eyes. "You know, you could've called."

"What?" Robby asked, baffled and amused by her sudden attitude.

"You could've called from your car. And I would've come to you. There's too many people in this mess. You wouldn't have found me with everyone holding up umbrellas." Eliza barked.

"Eliza. I just found you now. Here." Robby told her with a light-hearted grin.

Eliza shook her head, getting a grip. "Sorry. Um…You're right. Where's your car?"

Robby stood next to her overlooking the wave of rushing police officers. "What on earth happened?"

"You didn't hear that?" Eliza asked him.

"I only just stepped outside. I was going to check Inspector Gazi's until I –"

"A car bomb went off. It's a shame." Eliza told him.

"A car bomb!? Holy cow. We should go see-"

"Where's your car?" Eliza said cutting him off. Her heightened eyebrows and the slight cringe of haste told him that she wasn't interested in joining the fray. Seemed like she just wanted to get away.

Robby chuckled with a nod. His blush was unable to hide his attraction. Like a gentleman, he held the umbrella over her and escorted her half a block down the sidewalk away from the origin of disruption. His car was parallel parked on the street next to a rustic coffee shop. While she wondered if this was on purpose to entice her inside the shop, she couldn't help but grin at the sight of his car.

"Nice." She uttered.

Robby used a remote to unlock the doors. "Like it? It's a vintage 2186 Ichigo Splinter."

"Hmm... Same year I was born." Eliza revealed.

"Word? What are you nineteen? Twenty?" Robby asked.

"Closing in on twenty." Eliza quickly spit out, wanting to change the subject.

The silver metallic paint on Robby's two-door coup was classy. The reflection of the red, yellow, and green street lights on the rain covered streets mirrored off the side panels. The body of the car was streamlined and sat low to the ground. It had custom installed LED head and rear lights. The standard gauges were replaced with colored sky-blue gauges that measured not only the RPMs, fuel, speed and heating, but also the air intake, turbo, and suspension pressure. The black and grey leather seats had the imprints of roaring lions engraved just below the headrest. And as Eliza entered, marveling at the beautiful machine in its entirety, she noticed was a badge hanging from the hook above the rear view display screen.

"Car bomb. That's crazy, man." Robby uttered, still wanting to go check out the scene.

He carefully slid his wet umbrella behind the seat as he entered the car and saw Eliza staring at the badge. After closing his door and pressing a button to start the ignition, Robby explained. "Yeah. It brings me comfort. Reminds me of what my old man sacrificed."

"You need that to remind you?" Eliza asked.

Robby pondered. "No. Guess I don't *need* it. But still. You know…"

"I get it. I understand." Eliza told him with a nod.

Robby smiled as he returned with a mimicking nod of his own. Then, he turned on the windshield wipers and slowly pulled out of the parking spot. The music was already turned down, playing the latest contemporary pop songs. And as Robby maneuvered through the winding one-way streets heading west towards the district of Hyde Park, he kept glancing over at Eliza. Her nostalgic gaze recapturing some of the sights she used to take in as a child. The impressive Halo. The numerous overpass bridges and tunnels that made it feel like you were driving through a nest of roads.

Her fingers were interlocked and resting calmly in the lap of her tight jeans. Her figure. Her form and the sexy tone of her thighs were made evident as they pressed together with only her ankles crossed at the bottom. Robby's heart raced as her strawberry scented perfume filled his lungs. It was undeniable that he was attracted to her. But the thought of him ever thinking about asking her out again was out of the question. He acknowledged that he was completely out of Eliza's league. It was just best to assume so, he thought.

"So did you hear about Ybor last night?" Robby asked.

"Hmm?" Eliza turned to him with a raised brow.

Robby grinned. Even from his amateurish experience in investigating, he knew her response to be false. "Last night. Down in Ybor? The forums are buzzing with a hailstorm of rumors and speculations. There's even a couple of videos. Looks fake. But I dunno." Robby told her.

"Forums? What kind of forums?" Eliza asked.

"You know. Online forums. With these new jacked up laws, internet access is restricted to universities, a few wireless companies and certain Imperial owned buildings. But my laptop is equipped to steal their bandwidth and bypass satellite restrictions. Anyways. Online forums. I'm active on a few of them, actually. Anytime something new pops up in the underground scene, I hear about it. And last night... SOMEONE!" Robby said, with a wide grin of skepticism.

"Someone attacked a man whose description sounds remarkably similar to a one Braden Pierce. Even killed four of his bodyguards. That sounds like some heavy stuff, right?"

Eliza appeared shocked. She turned back to look at the rain bouncing off the tinted window. "Really?" She said, not so much as a question, but fascinated by the developments.

"Give me a break, Eliza. For someone with a deep grudge against the guy, it's surprising that you're not asking more questions." Robby told her.

Eliza turned back to lock eyes with him. The sudden intensity made Robby wonder if he had just offended her, if he had said too much. But she wasn't angry or unsettled by what he just said. She simply contemplated. With what she had planned, it didn't make sense to lie to him or keep him in the dark. Her intuition told her that young Robby would be willing to do anything for her, even though she knew so little about him. So…she took a chance. A stab in the dark. Come what may.

With a stoic stern gaze, Eliza spoke loud and clear so she wouldn't have to repeat herself. "That was me who attacked him last night. I killed those guards."

Robby's grin disappeared immediately. Like a strong magnetic pull, his attention suddenly turned straight to focus on the road in front of him. For some reason his right hand kept erratically jumping from the steering wheel to the gear shift.

Eliza smirked with a mild tone of sadism. "Problem, Robby?"

Robby chuckled nervously and slightly cocked his head in a nervous tick. "Nah, Eliza. I gotta say…I mean…Your sense of humor is a slight bit…You know, kind of out there."

"The girl who attacked Braden was wearing black. She had long curly blonde hair. Remind you of someone?" Eliza asked as she twirled a finger through her locks.

Robby's heart began to pound. His mind backtracked to figure out if he had even told her that it was a girl who attacked Braden. Slowly, the silver Splinter pulled up to a yellow light that was turning red. After stopping, Robby impulsively turned on his stereo system to play punk rock music that was synched on his cell phone. The blaring music was enough to distract anyone from such concerning thoughts.

Whilst sitting there parked at the red light, Robby kept his eyes forward even though Eliza had shifted her body so that both shoulders faced him. Without saying a word, she slowly lifted her left hand to pull down on the collar of her blouse. The sudden large contrast of her tan skin to the dark blue blouse she was wearing was enough to get his attention. There was a thick reddish vertical bruise on her right clavicle. It was the bruise she received from blocking Braden's strike just before she was forced through a frosted glass panel.

"Oh…" Robby said in a strained whisper as his eyelids opened full capacity.

…

BEEP BEEP!!!

The two honks were from the car behind them. The light had been green for well over ten seconds. The silver Ichigo Splinter peeled off in a mad tire-screeching dash with Robby punching the pedal to the floor.

Eliza sat back in her seat, clutching the door handles and bracing herself for any kind of impact. "ROBBY!!!"

"HOLY SHIT! How did you? You killed four bodyguards? Black-fucking-Creek security guards?! He's seen your face. Are you crazy? What in the actual fuck is wrong with you?"

"Robby! You slow this car down! Right now!" Eliza shouted over the music, accidentally slurring her "Rs" with spit.

"Eliza. Are you crazy? You could've been killed. Braden…Let me tell you something. Braden isn't some run of the mill street killer. I know this sounds crazy, but there's this thing. Alright! There's this thing called the Furyx Gene. All right? And it's just a rumor, but they say once you take it…"

"It's all you need?" Eliza said, cutting him off. "Your senses become heightened. You become abnormally stronger and faster. Your skin is durable enough to deflect small caliber shells. Also, you don't need so much sleep. You heal faster. You only need to hear and see things once to commit it to memory. I'm sure your friends on the forums didn't tell you that last part, did they?"

Robby's jaw dropped as he turned to her with a comical gawk. Eliza gasped. "Robby Robby Robby!!!"

At 55 mph, the sports car was speeding head on towards a group of sixteen elderly nuns walking over a pedestrian crossing. Eliza reached over with one hand to grab the top of the steering wheel. As Robby instinctively applied the brakes, she was able to bypass his grip on the wheel, maneuver the car to the right to jump over a curb, and swerve into a green-top basketball park. It came to a complete stop in the center of a court while the high school team running it was safely enjoying a recess on the bleachers, each of them staring at Eliza and Robby as if they had three heads.

Ignoring the mayhem and screaming nuns who were all shouting ungodly expletives, Robby finally asked, "Eliza, how do you know all of that? Most people haven't even heard of the Furyx Gene, including Police Superintendent Lobos."

Eliza's nerves were racked as she combed her fingers through her hair. "I've had the Furyx gene in me since I was fifteen. I won't tell you how or why, so don't ask. Honestly because even I don't fully understand that one."

Robby was nervous with a thick glob in his throat. He didn't know what to make of it all. When he told her that Braden would probably be at Club Havoc, he was expecting that she'd go to just scope him out. Not engage him in a full frontal assault. Even when he began the conversation on the subject, he was expecting her to have some juicy news that his forum friends lacked. But still…as a bystander.

After a twenty-minute drive with messed up suspensions, the light rain had calmed down to a light drizzle. Robby and Eliza were now in Oldsmar district, a small town located north of the bay and far from towering buildings of downtown Tampa. It was a more rural district with more trees and smaller historical establishments that have been around for well over two hundred years. The traffic was mild and there weren't so many sirens or helicopters. It was the eye of the hurricane.

"The place is up here." Robby told her.

The silver Splinter was pulling into a remote business center. Most of the abandoned cement factories, auto garages and textile mills still had a foreclosure and for sale signs on them. But after the war, Tampa business moguls found it cheaper to buy resources from rural towns outside the major cities. One warehouse was particularly large, about the size of a high school gymnasium. It was isolated on the L-shape corner of a street block with two ways to approach or leave. When Robby pulled up to the front of the warehouse, there was already a faded yellow car parked in one of the twenty-five spaces.

There was a prolonged awkward silence between the two even after he parked. Eliza revealed more than enough. So she was waiting on his approval or disapproval. And yet…he said nothing, but wore a foreboding look of dread and gloom. It was a weight upon Eliza's heart, and she'd much rather preferred him calling her crazy and be done with it.

A large splash reached Eliza's knees as she exited the car and placed a boot on the pavement. She was too preoccupied with Robby's thoughts to care. Right when she was finally about to come out and ask the warehouse's front entrance opened up. A realtor dressed in a long red and gray raincoat was leaning out of the doorway.

"Oh! There you are. I knew the rain would hold you up, Robby. Dreadful conditions!" Nikki said with a wide inviting smile.

Pulling on the tip of his cap with a sullen gaze, Robby explained. "Ms. Nikki and I go way back. She was friends with my mom when she used to live in Miami."

"Come Come, Robby! Shom-on! Let's get out of this horrid weather. Ewe!"

Approaching her late forties, Miss Nikki was a short pudgy woman with long brown hair and a heavy dose of makeup foundation. A warm soul nonetheless.

With obvious silent tension, Eliza and Robby crept up the warehouse like a pair of kids who were waiting to get scolded by an adult. But as soon as they entered, their attention took on another focus. The place was a wide-open space, dimly lit by lamps that hung from long chains from the forty-five foot ceiling. It was empty and barren. The concrete cinder block walls were painted black. The floors were covered with a quarter inch layer of commercial grade black rubber matting. And in one corner of the rectangular shaped warehouse was a staircase that led up to a mezzanine loft above the bathrooms and water fountains. Eliza walked up the staircase slowly sliding her hand along the rough splintery wood railing. Tuning out Ms. Nikki's nonstop chatter about its history, she had already fallen in love with the place.

"So, is this the friend you were telling me about Robby?" Nikki said as she playfully shouldered into Robby's.

Eliza turned and looked down the stairs to Robby, also awaiting his answer. The young man in the red baseball cap was staring off into space, still trying to put everything into perspective until, within seconds, he finally turned to Nikki…then to Eliza… and finally said…

"Yes. She's the friend I was telling you about." He said with a warm smile.

Eliza returned his answer with a warm smile of relief, finally able to move past the awkward tension.

"Good! Good!" Nikki said before letting out a hearty chuckle that mildly sounded fake. "Elizabeth is it?"

Eliza responded with a nod.

Well, as you can see. This space is very quiet and isolated from the hustle and bustle from the fast paced city atmosphere. It's right dab in the middle of Tampa and St. Pete's districts so you shouldn't have a problem getting around on the Halo rails. Since it's out of the way so you can basically do anything. Use it for all purposes. You can even start your own dance academy in here. You know with all the programs the Provisional Emperor has set up, it shouldn't be hard to receive some kind of grant or a loan." Nikki told her.

"Yeah, how are you gonna afford this?" Robby asked her as he leaned on the banister from the bottom of the loft steps.

Eliza was looking around upstairs in the medium office-sized loft. The view out the window to the south was nice, but she had already made up her mind to get it tinted. She heard their question and quickly walked toward the safety rail to address them.

"My inheritance. It seems you spent yours on that remote control car out there. I'll spend mine on this place." Eliza said with a smirk.

"Blahahaha…remote control car, she says!" Robby laughed sarcastically. "Girl's got jokes."

"She's hot." Nikki whispered to Robby.

Robby face quickly transformed to that of dread as he whipped his index finger towards the old woman. "Please don't whisper. She can hear you. Like, freaking supersonic hearing."

Nikki laughed out loud again. "You two are adorable!"

Eliza jumped over the loft's ledge railing and landed safely on the floor below. It was a twenty-foot drop that amazed both Nikki and Robby. "I'll take it. Where do I sign?" She asked.

"Oh! Well, I didn't bring the paper work. I wasn't prepared for-" Nikki began.

"That's okay. I'll stop by your office to sign it later. Robby and I actually have somewhere we need to be." Eliza told her as she approached them.

"We do?" Robby asked, almost as surprised as Nikki.

"Mm-hmm… We need to hit the Medici library to get online." Eliza told him.

"Eliza, I told you. With my laptop I can get internet access anywhere." Robby reminded.

"Even to international websites?" Eliza asked.

"Baby… Anywhere." Robby proudly boasted.

"Oh yeah? Well that's even better then. There's a spot I want to take you. I haven't been there in a while." Eliza told him while childishly poking his shoulder.

Robby sighed with apprehension. "Damn. Now what?"

Eliza put her hands on his shoulders and gently shook him. "Robby. Sometimes you just need to…Shut up! Now let's go." Eliza walked past him toward the door.

The smell of her strawberry-scented perfume was enough to knock down his wall of concern and apprehension. Lowering the tip of his hat to shroud his gaze from Ms. Nikki, he simply followed along.

Nikki stood in the doorway and watched as Eliza and Robby walked toward the low-riding Ichigo Splinter. "Give me the keys." Eliza demanded.

"Dude. You're not driving ma car. I don't care what you think you can do." Robby barked back, laughing at the absurdity of her request.

Eliza laughed. "All right. Well, you'll have to follow my directions."

"What do you think I've been doing all day!?" Robby playfully barked back.

"My goodness. When did you suddenly become a whiner?" Eliza laughed as she opened her door.

"The second I found out you were crazy." Robby answered before entering his own.

Nikki smiled warmly as the Splinter pulled off down the wet roads, still on busted suspensions. A moment later, with her imagination running wild, she let out her annoying laugh again. For Nikki, it was all too adorable to be contained.

Chapter 12 – Reminiscing the Last Rebellion

Oldsmar Park was a large grassy field in front of an old pavilion. The pavilion was an old white and blue outdoor stage made of brick and cement and covered by a large canopy. The back of the stage faced a long simple wooden pier that protruded out over the murky waters of safety harbor, a northern extension of the Bay of Tampa. It was getting late in the afternoon and the rain had dissipated enough to bring in the day's first golden sunrays that were visible in the breaking cumulonimbus clouds. Robby's metallic Splinter approached and came to a slow halt in the lot next to the stage.

Robby opened his door and got out to look around. He had never been there before and found a certain tranquility about the area. The pavilion was a good three hundred yards away from the nearest house and there were only four single story houses in sight. It was the smooth relaxing sound of nature that eased Robby. In the busy heart of Tampa, all you'd hear were the sounds of heavy traffic, public announcements, ads and endless chatter from people and their smart phones. Thus, Robby took in the brisk salty sea air, the squawking seagulls, and the smooth sounds of the tide coming in. It was different and beautiful.

"How do you know about his place?" Robby asked.

Eliza checked her cell phone. Gazi had called her three times but she didn't feel like speaking to him, let alone, checking his voice messages.

"I told you. I used to live around here. I have an old childhood friend who lives pretty close by. Aida… I actually need to get in touch with her at some point." Eliza said after silencing her phone. She tossed it in her seat before closing the car door.

"Oh. Did you want to pay her visit later?" Robby asked as he zipped up his yellow and black thick padded coat.

Eliza shook her head. "Nah. It's been a while since I've seen her but she's the type who asks a lot of questions. I don't have time for that right now. Get your laptop and meet me over here."

Robby scoffed at the way she casually gave out orders. He didn't want their relationship to start off with him being her lackey subordinate, but he followed her instructions nonetheless. Eliza walked toward the steps leading up to the stage of the pavilion. The smooth yet sandy stage floor was relatively dry. She looked for an electrical outlet and found it along the wall upstage.

"Over here!" She called out while squatting down. She wiped her hand over the outlet to make sure there was no moisture.

"Damn it's cold out." Robby complained as he approached carrying his book bag.

Eliza shot him a look. "Someone suggested a nice cozy library. But someone else wanted to brag about their precious laptop."

"Yeah, about that. Don't you think you might want to lay low, after last night? What if we run into someone who recognizes you? I heard they have hackers that dive into the city's CCTVs."

Eliza sighed in annoyance. "Just get your laptop out. Trust me Robby. When there's a need to be worried, I'll let you know. If you saw me in action you wouldn't be so concerned." She said as she stood up.

Robby sat down Indian style on the bare stage floor, disregarding its sand dirty condition. Eliza walked toward a railing overlooking the water. The cool wind blew through her hair and despite the cold stinging her eyes, she found it all so soothing. Robby glanced up at her while he was waiting for his laptop to boot up. He couldn't help but see her as some classical figure from a painting. She stood so tall and straight with perfect posture. The way she had her hands in the pockets of her long overcoat hoodie that basically looked like a cloak, she bore the look of a prisoner who had seen her share of tragedies. He knew what it was like to lose a parent to the Pierce, but he couldn't comprehend the difference between their losses. Robby wondered what it was about the death of Eliza's father that made it much worse to bear.

Eliza caught his stone-grey eyes fixated on her. Her long blonde hair was caught in the wind and streaked across her face. "You have it up?" Eliza asked as she used her fingers to comb her hair back and pull it into a ponytail.

"Eliza…" Robby began, no longer able to hold back his concerns.

"You have me out here finding you empty warehouses that's out of the way. You come out and tell me that you tried to kill Braden and actually did slaughter four of his security guards. I'm a part of this whether you like it or not… But at least tell me what you want to do. Because I think it's rude and insulting if we get off to a start where you're treating me like some mindless pawn. Don't get me wrong, I think you're beautiful. And in some twisted sense that I need to have checked out, I admire how bold you are. But I can't have you treating me like some lackey. I won't put up with it. And I honestly don't think I deserve to be treated that way."

Eliza smiled and thought he was an adorable antiquated dork for being so straightforward, yet scared out of his mind. She honestly did want to tell him everything and saw him as someone more valuable than he probably knew. But she didn't want to overwhelm him. So she pondered deeply over what to say, turning back to look at the choppy waters. She clasped her fingers together as she rested her forearms on the chipped blue-painted metal railing.

"Robby... You and I aren't alone. I think you yourself told me this. I bet you and I are a dime a dozen when it comes to scars left behind by the syndicate. And you're right. You don't deserve to be treated like a pawn. Which is why I *am* trusting you. Not only to keep everything I'm about to say to yourself, but to believe me. To believe that I'm not fooling around here. I know that...I know that what I'm setting out to do is gonna make me a hypocrite of sorts. Its gonna make me seem selfish. But I'm prepared for it. I've accepted it."

After hearing her declaration, Robby strained to exhale as if he had just been submerged into subzero temperatures. He nodded. "I promise, Eliza. If you trust me, I'll trust you. That's how this is gonna work. It's the only way it's gonna work."

Eliza nodded as she approached. His heart nearly stopped as she squatted down so that she was at eye level with him. The quiver in his cheeks intensified as she reached inside her coat and pulled out the green-leaved sheathed short katana that was resting along her lower back.

"Yo... Were you wearing that this whole time? Even at the police station?" Robby asked.

She held Ivy up with one hand on the sheath and the other on the hilt. Then, she slowly released the blade, the sleek clean steel casting a reflection on Robby's eyes. "Robby, I plan to take down the syndicate. Not just Braden Pierce. But the godfather Isaac himself." Eliza said with intense solidarity.

Robby's eyebrows furrowed involuntarily. While he did take her seriously in the sense that she believed she could do it, he just couldn't grasp the fact that it was possible. Eliza noted his skepticism but wasn't offended. She quickly returned the blade to her sheath and stood up.

"Well? What are your thoughts?" She asked as she walked back to the railing.

"Well…I mean…Eliza." Robby said with an uneasy smile, trying to tactfully choose his words.

"Well what? Spit it out? I want to know your opinion on this. Honestly." She told him.

Robby thought to himself in a bewildered gaze momentarily before mouthing the word, "okay". He then went to work on his laptop, clicking open a web browser and going directly into a search engine.

"I mean. What do you plan to do? Just waltz into their main building and start killing everyone?" Robby asked.

Eliza's eyebrows quickly bounced up and down. "I hadn't thought about something that simple. But it is possible."

"AENN!" Robby sounded like a buzzer. "It's not possible. It's been tried before."

Eliza scoffed. "Bullcrap. Since when?"

Robby nodded to himself. "Thought so. You probably never heard of the Five Pillars have you? Surprising given the impact they made not only in Florida, but the Empire in general."

He reached into his book bag and pulled out a small apple sized black spherical device with a lens. He hooked the device up to the top of his laptop and pointed the lens towards a wall on the opposite side of the stage.

"If you're talking about the Five Pillars of Minority, I have heard of them. That was like what, ten years ago, right? They were a bunch of thugs killed in a shootout with the police. Why compare them to me?" Eliza told him.

"Yeah, No. That's what the media outlets reported they were. And everyone knows that history is written by the victors. Cause…You know…the news reports never fabricate. I say sarcastically. The Five Pillars of Minority were a prominent group originally based out of Miami. They were active when my Dad held office there, so I know everything there is to know about them. Those men were anything but thugs. They took on the syndicate and they did it without the help and protection of the Furyx Gene."

Eliza gave a casual roll of the eyes in response to his subtle indirect jab. Then she turned her attention to what he was projecting onto the wall. It showed five photos different men that he had up on a website.

Robby explained. "Meet the Five Pillars of Minority. A collection of five gangs, 80 men, wrapped into one entity. These were the five leaders, with no one holding more authority over the other. They were all the sons of already infamously deadly gang leaders, all based in Miami. They were ruthless, bold and on a freaking mission, man."

Eliza had seen their faces before, but it was back when she was a little girl. Neither her father nor Gazi ever spoke of them. She wondered why they weren't brought up as much if they made such an impact.

"Going from left to right, I'll introduce these handsome devils." Robby began. "On the far left there is Tetsuya Furuya. They were all leaders, per se, but Tetsuya was the main man calling the shots."

The photo shown of Tetsuya was taken a month before his death at the age of 24. Tetsuya was of Japanese descent, relatively tall, with short jet-black hair combed back into a pompadour. Just as the photo depicted, he was rarely caught without dark black sunglasses and his brown leather motorcycle jacket with a fur collar.

"Tetsuya was the man who founded the Five Pillars. His father was Masa Furuya, one of Isaac Pierce's toughest in-state rivals. This was back before a "syndicate" was even established. It was every gang for itself. The small fish get eaten by the larger fish type deal. While Tetsuya was studying abroad in Japan, Isaac's oldest son, Alberto came into Masa's restaurant and set fire to the place, burning it down. In that fire, Bertie killed Tetsuya's mom, his dad, his three younger sisters and his little brother. Tetsuya returned to nothing but desolation and tragedy. Not surprising that he would show impressive leadership skills in rallying the old gangs under his name and vowed to take the Pierce down." Robby explained.

"Next to him is a childhood friend and another son of a gang leader, Tien Tayu." Robby introduced.

The photo of Tien was also taken a month before his death at the age of 23. Tien was of mixed Korean-Chinese descent but American born. He had a lean athletic figure and wore a patch over his left eye with a Christian cross embossed on it. The eye wasn't missing, but he was color blind in one eye. Without the patch, it wouldn't take long for Tien to catch a sudden throbbing headache.

"When Tien's father was gunned down in a shootout with Boss Rosenberg's men in 2190, Tien took control of the gang and hid out mostly along the ruins of South Beach. He built a shelter for other orphans and abandoned youths. Tien was a masterful thief and skilled daredevil. According to my dad's profile, he was the levelheaded reasonable leader in the Five Pillars. My dad credits his organizational prowess as the reason why the Pillars had a near five year stint when they should've been wiped out the moment they reared their heads." Robby explained.

"In the middle there is Javier Cortez, simply known as Jay Cortez." Robby introduced.

The photo taken of Jay was close to his death at the age of 20. Unlike the other leaders, there were hundreds of photos of Jay as he was bit of a social media fiend and not as reserved. Jay was of Puerto Rican-Cuban descent, with athletically toned ivory colored skin and long wavy dark hair. In the picture, Jay was wearing a black tank top bearing multiple upper body tattoos. And he was smiling. A carefree toothy childish smile of someone you'd least expect to be a relentless fighter.

"Jay was the youngest leader in the Five Pillars. But even though he was young, he had a fiery spirit and was fearless. He didn't back down from anybody, not even Tetsuya. It's said that when they were younger, even though Tetsuya was fifteen and Jay was eleven. When Tetsuya dumped Jay's older sister and refused to call her again, Jay challenged him to a fight."

Robby let out a chuckle. "I'm telling you, Eliza. I grew up listening about their adventures. They were…they were something else. It was messed up when they died."

Eliza nodded, thoroughly entertained and grateful.

"Hold on, let me put on some music." Robby said before playing some edgy rock songs from a playlist. "Sets the tone for the story, ya know."

"That pretty boy beside Jay is Jack Koo Kim." Robby introduced.

Eliza nodded. "Yep. I've heard of him."

"Yeah, I bet you have. What woman hasn't? It's a dark humor joke, but for years, a lot of the Caribbean natives thought he was truly Satin the Devil. Not because he was evil, which he was. But because of his looks. You see, in the old Bible texts, they say Satin was originally an angel who was sent to earth and became a demon. Old movies and ancient literature depict Satin to be this ugly horned monster of a beast, when more plausibly, Satin who is said to be the great tempter, should actually be depicted to be one of the most attractive beings ever created. So anyone perceived to be too good looking with a dangerous stigma is affectionately known as a Satin. Get it?" Robby explained.

Eliza shook her head no, but picked up on what he was saying. "Basically, because Satin was an angel, just because he fell from heaven, it didn't make him ugly. He should still be beautiful." She confirmed.

Robby snapped his fingers. "Exactly! And since Satin was the greatest tempter of mankind, well, if history's taught us anything it's that the person with the best looks is often the one who people assume to be the good guy."

"Go on!" Eliza snapped at him.

Robby laughed. "Well, there you have Jack Koo Kim. The devil of South Beach."

The photo of Jack was taken months before his death at the age of 24. He was of Korean-American descent with long black hair, possessing the seductive slanted dark eyes of a geisha, but tall with broad shoulder. Jack's face showed the expression of someone harboring a grudge. But despite his malicious expression, even Eliza had to admit that there was something hypnotic about him. It subtly reminded her of someone else she knew.

"Jack's father was murdered when he was still a baby, but it was his mother that played a key role into shaping this bastard. His mother basically controlled the prostitution and escort service in Miami. So Jack grew up rich, extremely good looking and surrounded by women. I don't know about you, but if someone were to strip all that away from me, I'd go a little batshit insane too. Jack wasn't crazy, but he had a reputation as one of the most ruthless serial killers in the country. I once read that he killed a pair of twin brothers simply because they're names appeared in one of his girl's caller ID. He once decapitated a waiter at a restaurant because he was still eating when the waiter tried to take away his plate. He's the only one I have absolutely no respect for."

"Then this last one must be Casper." Eliza said as she approached the wall and examined the photo of Casper closely.

"Yep. Aka, the Grin-Demon. The only one still alive." Robby added.

Eliza turned to him with a puzzled look. "Still alive?"

"They never found his body." Robby pointed out.

"Yeah, but you'd think someone of his caliber wouldn't exactly stay hidden. With a name and a face like that." Eliza told him.

The photo of Casper was taken the same year his comrades were killed. He too was 24 at their time of death. Casper was of Samoan descent, ruggedly handsome with long curly hair almost the size of an afro. His brown eyes seemed to glow in the photo, almost as if they were colored orange. He had a ripped lean physique with two katana wrapped around his waist on a belt like the two guns a gunslinger would wear.

"Casper actually wasn't the son of a gang leader, but just a gang member. When his father died with no mom around, he grew up sort of the lone wolf type. Rumor has it that he was one of the best swordsmen around. And Casper and Jack were always at each other's throats, couldn't agree on anything. Casper was a notorious womanizer and didn't give a damn about authority. You put two alpha male womanizers in the same room and things are bound to get ugly." Robby told her.

With her hands in her coat pockets, Eliza examined the five leaders with a stern gaze. To her, they all seemed like promising men with a deep grudge and better reasons to go after the Pierce. And yet, they perished. She had heard about them, but not to the extent that Robby described.

"You were saying?" Eliza said as she turned to Robby with a look of concern. "You said that they tried walking through the front doors of the Pierce corporate building?"

"Oh yeah." Robby said as he stood up, stretched his legs and wiped off the back of his pants.

"The night they were finally done in. On East Pierce Street across from the corporate building where the museum now stands, it used to be a Pierce owned financial investment firm called Durant Gibbs Accounting. D.G. Accounting. On this particular day, the Five Pillars believed that Isaac would be in there. So after years of guerilla warfare, terrorism and tensions heightened by Jay's death, Tetsuya, Casper, Jack, and Tien launched a final all-out assault aimed for the Pierce's jugular. Their money." Robby explained.

"You won't find these facts on the internet and in this history books, but the Imperial officials know what happened. Officially…" Robby said, gesturing bunny ears with his fingers.

"Officially, Pierce corporate reps called the police and reported that the Pillars were holding several executives and brokers hostage in attempt to draw Isaac Pierce out of his safe room. SWAT then went in and after a barrage, the Five Pillars were no more."

"Hmph…So. Unofficially?" Eliza asked.

Robby started to grin. "Alright. So unofficially…And this might piss you off a little. Or make you happy. I don't know. There's no telling with you sometimes. Anyways unofficially… Isaac was never in the building. It was one of his sons, Charles I think. The Five Pillars captured Charles when they infiltrated the building. And when they got impatient with Isaac's stalling, Jack slit Charlie's throat. Only…it turns out that Charles wasn't the only Pierce in the building. He brought with him one of his younger cousins." Robby told her.

"Braden?!" Eliza blurted.

"Haha! No. But it was his little brother, Sean. He had to be around eight at the time while Braden was ten." Robby told her.

"So. Sean, evidently survived? What's so special about that?" Eliza asked.

"Who do you think killed Tetsuya Furuya? If Isaac himself didn't move an inch when his own son was murdered, do you think he'd risk anything to save little snot nosed runt like Sean?" Robby asked her while wearing a long grin.

Chills were sent down Eliza's spine. She turned around and took another look at Tetsuya's photo. Tetsuya was the cement holding the Five Pillars together. Someone of his caliber had to have experience, charisma, and considerable skill as a fighter.

"No! There's no way!" Eliza whispered.

Robby heard the whisper and nodded. "Braden showed his potential way before he intruded into your world. Unless we or somebody does something. I think Braden may well be on his way to overshadowing Jack's reputation as the most prolific serial killer."

Eliza shook her head in disbelief. "There's no way Robby. That's bullshit. Braden's the same age as us, and he didn't even have the Furyx Gene back then. Right?"

"That's right." Robby confirmed.

"Then how in the hell could he have taken down the Five Pillars? That doesn't even sound credible! It's ridiculous!" Eliza demanded to know.

"Easy…I never said he took down the Five Pillars. I'm saying he killed Tetsuya. According my dad's statements given by credible anonymous sources, in an attempt to end the Five Pillars once and for all, Isaac ordered the building to be burned down even when Sean was still held captive. The only one crazy enough to risk his life to save Sean was his older brother. There used to be footage from inside the building that's locked in government archives. In several shots, Tetsuya was the one holding Sean. It looked like he was protecting Sean if you can believe it. I know with stricter gun laws it's rare for kids to pull a trigger and kill a man. But if you know your way with the blade, taught from an early age the way Braden was, you don't need strength to stick a razor sharp point through someone's back."

Anger gripped Eliza. It seemed like every time she felt like she had some advantage over Braden, she'd find out that there was still more depth to him. "So what happened to the other members?" Eliza said as she intensely gazed at the photos.

"Well. After Sean was rescued. A fire did engulf the place with many of Isaac's own men trapped inside. Tien's body was found riddled with bullets. Pieces of Jack's body were found torn apart through the rubble. Authorities suspect that his body was on the roofs helipad before the building collapsed. There were, again, anonymous sources that claim to have seen Jack fighting with Casper as flames surrounded them. Haha. Even as their world came tumbling down, those two were still going at it. But Casper's body was never found."

…

The sun was setting. Street lamps were gradually lighting up around the pavilion and the golden glow from the Halo could be seen in the distance. The highlight of dark blue clouds were still visible in the horizon as they rolled east. Robby turned off his computer and put it in his book bag. After carefully zipping it up, he looked over to Eliza. Behind the stage, on the metal railing overlooking the bay, she stood motionless in the same spot for almost five minutes.

Robby approached and put a hand on her shoulders. "Eliza. I'm not saying it's impossible. I'm just saying it's been tried. When you're at the top, you gotta figure they've had their share of enemies with more resources and manpower than us. What are you gonna do that's different from the rest them? That's all I'm saying."

Eliza nodded before exhaling sharply.

"Come on man. It's getting cold out here." Robby told her as he started to walk away.

"You go on ahead. I'll catch up with you later." Eliza said, her eyes still fixed on the surface of the bleak waters.

"But you don't have a ride. Come on, you can't possibly make it to the nearest Halo station…"

"Thank you." Eliza said, cutting him off. She grabbed the hood of her coat and slowly brought it over to cover her head. "The cold doesn't bother me. I like views like this. I'll be fine."

Robby sighed and felt guilty. He didn't want to leave her, but wasn't sure how she'd felt if he stayed. A damned if you do, damned if you don't situation. So reluctantly, he turned to walk back to his car. After taking a couple steps, he turned around. "Eliza, seriously. I'm sorry if I…"

"Robby!" Eliza barked sharply. "You're fine. Thank you. I'm not mad at you. Everything you did today has been really helpful. I mean it. I'll call you soon."

Robby shook his head in disbelief. "You're not gonna change your mind about this are you? You still want to take on the syndicate."

Eliza didn't respond. Her back was turned on him with a wind blowing through the tails of her coat. But she stood solid like a watchtower.

Robby sighed. "Well, if it makes you feel any better. They don't say this in any report, but from my dad's profile of Tetsuya Furuya…In my opinion, I think he let Braden kill him. I don't think Tetsuya even put up a fight. It was Jack's idea to kidnap Sean and I bet Tetsuya was against it. In the five years the Five Pillars have waged war against the Pierce, they've never killed women or children. Maybe that small bit of humanity was Tetsuya's folly. I just want you to ask yourself something. Is it worth it? At the sake of sacrificing your own humanity, is it worth it to take on the syndicate? Because that's what it's gonna take."

Robby said his final thoughts on the matter and headed for his car without any regrets. Eliza listened as it pulled off. She knew Robby was right about a lot of things, but she resented him for comparing her to Braden or the Five Pillars. For two hours, she let the icy sea air rush through and cool her heated veins.

The clouds that brought rain earlier in the day moved on to make way for a clear view of the crescent shaped moon. After a while, she lowered her hood and released her long hair to comb her fingers through it. Almost as if she were having a conversation with herself, she nodded in understanding. Robby's opinions were understandable. She couldn't blame him for not putting 100% trust in her from the get-go. It would be foolish if he did.

"Indivisualism is not an organization, but a movement." She recited aloud to herself. "It's a sense of feeling, a self-acknowledgement of freedom from traditions and historical precedence. An indivisualist is in control of their own world and blames no other human or entity for their own mistakes."

The words enrich her and reinvigorated the goals she made four years earlier. "This is my life. Sacrifice my humanity? Who's to say I ever even had any?" She said out loud with strong conviction.

Suddenly a ring tone of Karl Jenkin's "Palladio" played from her cell phone. Robby had left her phone on the ledge of the stage before he took off. Eliza walked over and picked it up. Sure enough, it was Robby calling her. With a strong sense of conviction, she picked it up, prepared for whatever other helpful words of wisdom he wanted to spew out this time.

"Hello." She answered calmly.

"Hey. I just wanted to say…" Robby began before pausing briefly.

Eliza waited.

"I just wanted to say. No matter what, I'm with you. I said that before, but I just wanted to assure you that no matter what I'm still with you." Robby told her.

"Are you sure?" Eliza asked.

After a brief pause and a deep sigh, "Yes." Robby responded firmly.

"Then meet me tomorrow at the library." Eliza told him as she looked up at the moon. "We have invitations we need to send out."

Chapter 13: The Assembly...

It was a Monday afternoon with sixty percent cloud coverage. The last week of summer break before the fall semester began. Robby was huffing and puffing across the nearly vacant campus lawns of the Medici heading towards the Ennis Coburn Library building. He was supposed to be there by three but got held up in a heated debate with one of his online forum buddies. As per usual, he was covered in one of his trucker hats and wrapped in his yellow and black padded coat with his backpack slung over one arm.

As he came bursting through the front doors he startled the senior student clerk at the check-out counter. Normally she'd scold such a hasty student, but with Robby being one of the few students who came by that day, she simply shot him a stern look. Robby smiled apologetically with a tip of the hat before hurrying past her and down the hallway.

The building itself was a massive state of the art four-story structure. You could reach the floors by either two pairs of elevators in the lobby or an art deco style stairwell that was stationed in the corner of the cafe. The walls of north face of the library were made of glass and showed the peaceful scenery of a large pond, surrounded by expensive landscaping designs of palm trees and a bicycle path. The first floor contained the fiction, media rentals and a café. Robby was supposed to meet Eliza in the café. Since the café was closed until the semester started, he had the whole floor of red eclectically designed tables and lounging chairs to himself.

Being that he was fifteen minutes late, Robby was surprised to find no sign of Eliza. He picked a table that was near a window and close to the stairwell. Going through the motions, he pulled his laptop from his book bag and plugged it into a floor-implanted outlet. He then took off his thick padded coat and folded it over the back of the chair. For a moment, he wished the café was opened because he could really use the caffeine.

After taking a seat in front of his computer, he took his smart phone from his pocket and checked it for any missed calls. There weren't any. He then briefly contemplated on whether he should call and let Eliza know that he was there before dismissing the thought with a chuckle. The first thing he did on his laptop was got some music going. Funneling through dozens of pre-made playlists, he picked the inspirational new age instrumentals of one of his favorite artists from Japan, Yuki Kanto. The first song was a smooth blending arrangement of light synths and string orchestra.

As soon as he put the music on he felt more at ease and could care less if Eliza was late or not. He began opening up web browsers, dead set on finishing his debate with the forum member he argued with earlier. And just as he started typing in the website's address, he heard the hard boot-on-tile footsteps descending from the stairs behind him. With a sigh of relief, he looked up to see Eliza carrying a cooler and a set of books. She was wearing brown boots, khaki pants and a long white form-fitting buttoned blouse that draped down almost to the length of her knees. All under her hooded green overcoat, of course.

"There you are. I was about to call you." Robby said.

In one arm, Eliza was carrying eight thick hardback books in a stack with the top book opened so she could somehow read while she walked. In her other hand, she was carrying a cooler down by her waist. Robby instinctively stared at her like she was a rogue android as she approached his table with the grace and elegance of a princess even though her attention was clearly focused on the book. He couldn't help but shake his head in disbelief. Without breaking stride with her reading, she casually put the cooler down on the floor, grabbed the book she was reading, and then set the other books softly down on the table. Out of curiosity, Robby thought it would be a good idea to lean under her hand to see the title of the book she was reading. But suddenly, she closed the book and dropped it spine first on his face.

"Ouch!" Robby muttered. He recoiled back in his seat while holding his nose.

"Oh! I'm so sorry, Robby! What were you doing?" Eliza said as she squatted to pick the book up from off the floor.

"Damn, dude. That kind of hurt." Robby complained with a forced chuckle.

Eliza smirked. "Well, that's what you get for being so nosy."

"Wow. Guess I kind of soft-balled that joke in for ya." Robby muttered.

"Here." Eliza said, setting the book down in front of him.

"Shinsengumi?" Robby read, surprisingly pronouncing the word properly.

"That's right. I read about them a lot during my studies abroad." Eliza said as she took off her green coat and laid it over the back of a lounge chair.

"So what was it? Or do you want me to sit here and read all about it?" Robby asked as he perused through the text for something interesting to pop out.

With her fingers clasped above her head, Eliza reached up as high as she could to stretch out her arms and back. The eruption of blush in Robby's cheeks was inevitable even though he could only throw lightning fast glances her way. That form-fitting shirt she wore really accentuated her firm bust. The natural light pouring through the windows gave her blonde hair a silver glow. Her emerald green eyes, almost magically, seemed bigger and brighter. Oblivious to Robby's racing heart and jittering fingers, Eliza casually opened the cooler and unloaded an assortment of sliced apples and oranges.

"Back in the 1860s, while the United States was going through the Civil War, Japan was dealing with their own internal strife, albeit caused from the State's influence. Or rather the Western Influence." Eliza explained.

"Sonno Joi! Revere the Emperor and Expel the western barbarians! This was the general sentiment that flooded the major cities of Kyoto and ancient Edo. Acts of murder and violence spread rampant through the streets and in broad daylight. With the government divided between pro-imperialists and shogunate loyalists, the innocent people, the bystanders were caught in the crossfire. And from the ashes of despair and strife, the Shinsengumi rose to the call." Eliza said with an added inspirational flare.

Robby chuckled at her enthusiasm. "So what? They were a…"

"Militia. A group of dedicated soldiers who came together for a common purpose. This is what I want to create." Eliza told him.

As Robby continued to peruse through the pages, Eliza stood over him with a hand on her hip. The other hand was feeding her an apple. And as she chewed slowly on a mouthful of juicy goodness, she noticed a look of doubt gradually form on Robby's face. After a seemingly prolonged moment of silence, Eliza impulsively closed the book in front of him.

Robby laughed. "I was still reading!"

"You can read later. I've made up my mind. This is what we're gonna do, and we need to get to work. What music is this?" Eliza spoke rapidly with a tint of spice.

Robby stretched back in his chair, slightly inundated by the thought. "Uh...this is Yuki Kanto. She's a Japanese composer from the early 2000s if you can believe it."

"This is good. I like it. Did you want something to eat? Help yourself Robby." Eliza encouraged as she sat on the edge of the table beside him.

Then...for some odd reason, Eliza and Robby just sat looking at each other in awkward silence. Both could tell what the other was thinking just by their expressions. Eliza was skeptical about his level of commitment. With a condescending grin, his arms were crossed and his trucker hat was pulled down. Robby flat out wondered about her mental stability. In a comical sense, he was thinking to himself that she was a possessed, stubborn, truculent bitch who just could not be swayed. And with a sudden tilt-head happy eye-smile, Eliza started thinking to herself how satisfying it would feel to slap that lop-sided grin off of his face.

Robby's arms finally untangled from their folded position to reach for an orange slice. Eliza's eyes followed his hand as it slowly reached for it. She knew he was taunting her with his intentional cautious slow motion, but she continued smiling and blinked heavily at him. The weird uneasy tension took its toll and caused Robby to erupt in laughter.

"Well damn!" Robby said with a smile, barely containing his laughter. "Where do we start, commander?"

Eliza popped off the table and stretched her arms again, this time out to the sides. Robby grew bolder, this time staring at the outline of her bra straps through the back of her white blouse as he bit into the orange. Then he noticed Ivy, the green and white ninja katana that was strapped to her lower back. The sight of it was a turn off.

"I need your advice on this one. I need to get a message out. I need it to be encrypted. An indirect message with an ambiguous but strong meaning." Eliza asked.

Robby thought to himself. "Like a mass ambiguous spam mail? Do you want it sent to everyone in the state?"

"No. Not the state, but more so the Tampa and Miami area. And I don't want this to go to just anyone's e-mail. What I'm looking for are people with a law enforcement or military experience. My own personal ronin. Wandering samurai." Eliza stressed.

Robby nodded. "Hmm…This could be interesting. It's been awhile. But last year when I created my own forum to debate the similarities between Greek mythology and the old Biblical religions, I sent out a press release that targeted only adults with a degree in Theocratic studies. It's a one of a kind press release displayed by an html-20 scripted webpage that I wrote and designed myself."

Robby was about to type on his keyboard to pull up the webpage when he suddenly stopped. "Eliza. You really are gonna owe me for all this. If the ICSA finds out about this, I could go away for a long time."

"ICSA?" Eliza asked.

"Imperial Cyber Security Agency. I'm not even supposed to have mobile internet access, let alone sending out network spiders to comb through the firewalls of over two million personal IP addresses."

Understanding only a tenth of the gravity involved in the risks Eliza sincerely walked over to put a hand on his shoulder. "I won't forget it Robby. I really do owe you the world."

"Damn straight. Hang on. Let me pull up the program I used the last time I did this." Robby told her as he began typing away on his keyboard, opening up programs left and right, entering passwords with his own personal keyboard hot keys.

Eliza continued to walk toward the windows until only her bracelet covered wrists were exposed to the shade's edge of the light. The large pond in the library's park was beautiful. A multicolored fountain geyser shot up to twenty feet in the center of it. Eliza's crystal clear green eyes honed in on the other side of the pond. A cluster of golden-brown mallard ducklings was following their mother in an adorable stroll around the banks. It was bittersweet for Eliza to see such a thing. The antipathies that seethed through were a harbinger of regret. And regret almost always brought abhorrence.

"I got it." Robby said, turning around to look at her. "You know what you want to say in this e-mail?"

Eliza soft eyes gradually began to well up, but she didn't shed a single tear. "I know exactly what I want to say. Are you ready?"

Robby nodded. "Just tell me what's on your mind and don't worry about me keeping up."

Eliza massaged her face aggressively with her hands before jumping up and down to shake off the rigid tension. "All right. Here goes…" She instructed him to type everything she mentioned verbatim, including the ums, ahs and brief pauses. And with that, she began.

"Ladies and Gentlemen. This message is a brazen declaration to state that the fabled Pierce Syndicate that has plagued and terrorized our home for so long does indeed exist. Those who have set out to prove this notion have since perished. Those who try to stand up against their corruption have been wiped from the face of this earth. The people know who the villains are. They have faces. They have names. These killers walk the streets in plain view just like everyone else, but no one does anything to stop them. People are mugged, beaten and killed every day and no one intervenes. Rapists and handlers prey on women and children with absolutely no fear of repercussions. People disappear. They're kidnapped. They're killed for their organs, their money, and their possessions. And it all goes on, business as usual."

"So this message goes out, not to victims, but to the survivors. Survivors covered with scars that still hurt and tear at us each and every day. Scars that can't be ignored. Scars that can't be healed. Scars inflicted by this so-called syndicate that has been allowed to grow and expand over the decade until now. Their very existence seems synonymous to both society and universal law. Every true indivisualist will agree that something needs to be done. An indivisualist, as defined by Reginald Harvey's August the 18th."

She turned towards the window and gazed softly at the family of ducks. "I am like you. I too, have lost someone close and dear to me. A vicious murder committed boldly right before my very eyes. But I was too young, too incompetent to do anything about it."

"Like you, I've waited. I've waited for the legal justice system that my father died believing in. I've waited for the justice system to make due on its purpose for being. The reason why laws even exist! But in the years that have past, I've learned that criminals seem to have more rights than the victims. Law enforcement officers are not equipped to deal with this problem. Too many rules inhibit the length of their reach. Too much freedom is being taken advantage of and its shielding the wrong element. So if you can't beat em, join em! This is the mentality that seems to percolate through the ranks, ostracizing the few good, honest cops who risk their lives just to stay clean."

Eliza's eyes began to swell as she approached the window. She folded her arms to hug herself and unwittingly started to dig her nails into her triceps. "This problem isn't ephemeral. It won't go away with time or tolerance. It will only evolve and grow stronger. Become advanced and inundating. It's irritating, I know. The irritation that boils under your skin isn't something you can ignore. Those who try and accept it, end up miserable. They end up blaming the whole world instead of the obvious source of that aggravation."

"Why is that?!" Eliza suddenly cried out with overwhelming emotion. "The answer is right there in front of you, yet you choose to ignore it. Is it easier for you to do that? To go on living your life in denial? Pathetic! To blame the sorry state this world is in on a single man or entity is ridiculous. It's insulting to think that we the people are all just pawns to be manipulated by their will with no control of our own."

"The syndicate cancer has done enough damage to this city and to our lives. Things are the way they are because no one has the courage, the muster, the true grit to stand up and do anything about it. And this isn't for everyone. Most people would love to make a stand, but know they just aren't physically capable of it. This message isn't for those poor souls. And that's okay. I'll represent those strong hearted individuals in my mission to eradicate the syndicate. The ones I'm talking to are the ones who know deep in the depths of your hearts that you have the ability, you have the skill, you have the means to make a difference. But out of fear... you'd rather blend in with denial. Hide behind the concept of, it could be worse. Or, this isn't worth fighting for."

She turned to Robby and boldly declared with the verve and brio of a general rallying her troops. "So let me be the nail that sticks out! Let me be the thorn that jabs into the rib cages of the Pierce! I do not fear the worst because the worse has already happened! If you're reading my words and feel not fifty, not ninety, but one hundred and ten percent of the same octane that fuels me, then respond. I'll send further notice of where and when to meet. Because something must be done. We must stop the cycle and prevent others from falling prey to the same predator that has picked us apart. We have to prevent others from…becoming like us. Cold. Heartless vindictive creatures. Cynical. Incapable of thinking of anything else but the worst imaginable death and destruction for the syndicate. Surrounded by everyone and yet…still alone."

Robby was typing at least 150 words a minute to get everything down to the queue. When he finally stopped typing, he slowly turned to her before letting out a sharp exhale. Her back was turned on him as she gazed out the window. Her shoulders were raised. Her hands were balled tightly into a fist but she stood inert like piece of art.

The sun was setting. From Robby's position, the sunrays projected a reddish-orange aura around her. Gradually, Robby began to feel sorry for what he said to her the other day. To compare one person's pain to another was inexcusable on his part. After hearing her declarations, he was finally beginning to understand that he could never begin to imagine how much pain Eliza carried with her. Nor did he feel it polite to ask.

"Eliza…" Robby softly called out.

"Robby. Can you do me a favor?" Eliza suddenly said almost in a whisper.

Robby smiled. "Of course, Eliza. What is it?"

"Send me a playlist of those songs by Yuki Kanto. I want to remember it." She said before turning to him and putting on a warm smile of gratitude.

Robby nodded. "Is there anything else you want to add?"

"No. That should be enough. I hope it's enough." Eliza said as she fetched her green hoodie and started to collect her belongings. "Thanks a lot Robby, you're the best."

Robby nodded with a smile. "You think anyone will show?"

"Only the ones that matter. Come on. We got some shopping to do."

"Um…Shopping?" Robby asked as he lifted the tip of his hat to scratch his front bangs.

"We have to make our warehouse look like a headquarters for when our guests arrive." Eliza said with an exciting look of anticipation.

"Oh! Is that why you bought that warehouse?" Robby said, feeling silly by the fact that he just now figured it out.

Eliza chuckled as she started down the hall. "Come on!"

"Wait Eliza. Gee whiz." Robby uttered as he hurried to pack up his power cord and laptop.

…

Eliza's message went out as planned in Robby's encrypted press release. It was sent to the e-mail addresses over two hundred thousand of current and inactive military personnel and law enforcement officers in south Florida. Most ignored the message, thinking it was the ramblings of some college student posing as an activist who wanted to organize some kind of petition or rally. But then there were the few who saw the message as something else. The few who deciphered certain words like "indivisualist," "August the 18th," and the bold accusation in the "Pierce" running the syndicate…That sort of talk was dangerous, even if it was coming from a harmless college student. Some of the recipients knew and completely understood that whoever the sender was meant business.

On the very same night that the message went out, a ruggedly athletic white male in his mid-forties was just now finishing up grading papers for his high school students. He was working from his computer in the living room of his middle-class home while his two daughters watched cartoons on TV. A portrait of the family was hanging above the mantle. The portrait showed the man, his two children, and his wife. The wife was an Imperial Special Intelligence Agent whose mangled and half-eaten body had washed up on the shores of Daytona. She died investigating a pipeline of ammunitions being smuggled in through the Port of Jacksonville.

The widower was Brian Wells, also a former special intelligence officer six years retired. Reading Eliza's words rekindled a fire in his pious heart. He had his doubts as any experience lawman would. But after the words opened his eyes and flat out accused him of hiding…Brian Wells could no longer remain dormant. Brian Wells heard the call.

…

The morning after the message went out, a tall man was checking his e-mail on a smart phone while walking the across a street toward a church in a popular subdivision of northern St. Petersburg. The man was in his mid-thirties with the somewhat appearance of a natural albino. His dull blond hair was cut short. He had distinct cold blue eyes that looked like they were implants and his skin was as pale and white as talc. He was a former sniper for the Imperial Ranger Forces during the border wars with Mexico, but he went AWOL two years ago after a decade of service. While the man had planned to put the phone away after the first two sentences, he was completely hooked by Eliza's words toward those living in denial.

This man was known simply as Priest Edwin.

Dressed in a sharp yet modest black suit and tie, Priest Edwin entered the large stone church to see a sermon was already in progress. Senior citizens had come to hear the pastor's words, ironically subjected around the topic of forgiveness. Whilst silently keeping to the dimmer wings of the nave, Priest Edwin walked to his post that was the piano. The pastor gave him a quick nod of acknowledgment and continued with his preaching. Edwin could hear the pastor's clear boisterous voice, but it was Eliza's words that captivated his spirit. His head was up, but his gaze was down at the phone reading her message over and over again.

Priest Edwin heard the call.

…

Former SWAT captain James Slater was sitting behind a desk in the lower level garage of the Tampa Metropolitan Police Department. He was once revered as one of the most athletically gifted recruits to come out of the academy with high scores in hand to hand combat and tactical infiltration. But after the recent catastrophe at the Clearwater airport where Braden brought down Salazar's plane in midflight, Slater took the fall.

As if the death of four of his comrades wasn't enough, he was demoted from SWAT Captain to tending the armory registry desk in the department's garage. Keeping the disdain and burning frustration bottled up inside, reading Eliza's message was but a mild remedy. Clearly, he needed more of that brand of medication. It didn't matter what Eliza had in store, Slater was ready to do anything if it meant taking on the syndicate.

…

Finally, the last of the four main leaders who would eventually join up with Eliza was a drifter named Sinus. He walked amongst the slums of downtown Ybor where prostitution and biker gangs ran amuck. He was a lean figure with broad shoulders, wearing a rough and dirty blue jean jacket over a ragged burgundy hoodie. Sinus had his head covered by the hood, shrouding his already gloomy and mysterious appearance.

Entering his rough and noisy apartment building, Sinus had to shoulder his way through the congested stairway of Latino gangsters who all stared him down, only barely moving out of his way. Some even drew their daggers, taunting him to make a move. But Sinus had gone through the same routine every night for nearly two years and didn't fear death, pain, and least of all a bunch of gangsters whose only courage was measured by the amount of people they kept around.

Upon entering his apartment and closing the door, he turned on the den lamp and greeted a white Persian cat that kept crying for attention. Taking off his coat and hoodie, he revealed a muscular toned body with long fluid black hair. Sinus was in his mid-twenties bearing the slanted eyes and gentle smile of his Korean-American heritage. There was a Korean broadsword attached to his back, previously concealed by the jacket. He unhooked it cautiously and leaned it against a wooden desk that he had salvaged from a junkyard.

Sinus logged into his old outdated desktop computer and opened up Eliza's e-mail three days after she sent it. He was recently released from county jail after cutting the arms off of three druggies who were trying to rob an elderly storeowner. He spent most of his adult life in and out of jail and was secretly yearning for a higher calling to put his potential to good use. Through Eliza's message, he found it.

Robby sent the e-mail out on a Monday. Even though the window was tight, both Eliza and Robby agreed that they had to move fast. During the week Eliza and Robby spent almost every waking minute searching for and furnishing their Oldsmar warehouse with discount couch sets, desks, and outdated yet capable computer equipment. By Friday, it didn't exactly look like your state-of-the-art intelligence headquarters, but that's what they made it out to be. Eliza had turned the upstairs loft into an office while the empty space in front of the entrance doors was made to look like a lobby. The rest of the space that made up seventy percent of the warehouse still lay barren.

At the end of the week, Eliza and Robby spent their Friday night in the loft of the warehouse, deliberating over what to put in the last e-mail to those who responded to her first one. Eliza told Robby to send an e-mail instructing them to drive to the busy Channelside Halo train station and to pick up a flyer for "18th BBQ Wings" at an information kiosk near lost-and-found. After picking up this flyer, they were to hold onto it for a week before receiving another e-mail. This second e-mail instructed them to brush lemon juice on the back of the flyer, and then hold it under a black light.

The instructions to the Oldsmar warehouse were written in an invisible ink that Eliza made herself. The ink was made to have a four day delay before any evidence of it could even be detected. So anyone getting wise to run all kinds of test on it earlier than expected would be disappointed. Those people would most likely throw the flyer away. Thus, weeding out people who couldn't follow instructions or posed a threat to operations for being too hasty. In this second e-mail, guests were also instructed to bring documents to prove their identities along with a duffle bag full of any gear or weaponry they planned to use out in the field. Last but not least, Eliza made it clear that everyone who planned to attend should wear some kind of facemask that covered his or her faces from the bridge of the nose down.

Robby did as he was instructed. With the invitations sent out, Eliza cautiously meditated on everything she did during the two weeks, looking for any holes and any error in her plan. Whether she made a mistake or not, the wheels were in motion and there was no turning back. That alone, the idea of action finally being taken…it was a sensational excitement she had to conceal.

Saturday came on a rainy day. At 11:55a.m., the parking lot to the isolated warehouse in Oldsmar was filled to capacity with some having to park out on the street shoulders. Only one person was seen walking down the street as if he had just caught a bus ride, but then had to walk the rest of the way. Everyone sitting in their parked vehicles watched as the drifter approached. Their tension and apprehension towards the drifter was alleviated when he was close enough for them to notice that he was wearing a facemask.

The second the clocks hit twelve, the driver doors opened almost in unison. Sixty-eight individuals had shown up, all dressed warmly and wearing some variation of a mask that covered their faces from the nose down. It was exactly as Eliza dreamed it would be.

Inside the warehouse, Eliza sat high up on the now polished wooden ledge of her loft. She could hear the footsteps approaching through the music that played from her ear buds. She was dressed in what would become her normal crime-fighting attire.

Her black form-fitting multi-pocketed cargo pants donned a subtle light-green leaf design running down the course of each leg to reach her black combat boots. The pockets all carried some variety of ninjitsu gadget that she learned to make from Hideo. She was wearing an expensive all-purpose sports bra under her black tank top and a dark-green buttoned up shirt that exposed her clavicle bone. Accessories included both knee and elbow pads with insulated tactical combat gloves that had a plastic shielding over the knuckles…as if she needed it. Her face was covered by a sleek-black ventilated facemask that had the design of green flames embossed on it. As always, Ivy was tucked by her lower back, concealed inside a heavy-duty dark green hooded raincoat. It was the closest one she could find that looked like the one she'd casually wear to school.

Robby was sitting on the steps that led up to the loft directly in view of the front entrance. He was on his computer, hacking into several satellite feeds at once. He had to implant a stationed image into the feeds so that it appeared that there was no activity going on in or around the warehouse. He wasn't dressed as seriously as the others. He had already made it clear to Eliza that his position with the group was strictly for tech support, not field work. Eliza did, however, succeed in persuading him to wear a facemask until she was sure that she could trust all of the members.

"They're here." Eliza said aloud. Robby overheard and looked over to see Eliza still sitting with her back towards him, high up on the ledge of her loft. He smirked at the mysterious front she was projecting.

"Alright then. Satellite feeds are good. Nobody will suspect at thing." Robby told her.

Before he could receive some sort of acknowledgment from Eliza, the front doors opened. One by one, the guests began filing into the warehouse with an eerie soldierly silence. They were all large adults. Even with their facemasks, they all seemed intimidating and dangerous. Robby quickly closed his laptop and put it on the steps before coming down to meet them.

The guests looked around the warehouse, both anxious and cautious, mostly of each other. With everyone wearing facemasks, no one could judge the other. No one could discern if anyone was a friend or foe. If Robby had not spoken up when he did, no doubt a fight would break out in which most of the guests would've left the premises.

"Hello and welcome!" Robby announced with a slightly nervous shake in his voice, his eyes randomly bouncing from man to man. Everyone stood in place. All eyes were on Robby.

"Um…We're gonna wait about five more minutes…and then, and then, we'll get started. So just um…make yourselves comfortable." Robby told them.

Slater was the first to impulsively remove his facemask and drop his duffle bag with a hard thud on the floor. Some were taken aback by his sudden boldness. His dark eyes and thick lowered eyebrows wore a look of obvious disappointment as he barked. "Hold up! Now I know you ain't the one who organized this shit? Kid looks old enough to be in boy band. The fuck is this?"

James approached Robby, and without thinking twice, yanked the facemask off of him. "What's your name boy?"

No one noticed that Eliza was sitting up on the ledge of the loft. She had become agitated by Slater's tone and finally turned around to see who he was and what he was about. After a quick scan of the group, Eliza discerned that Slater was one of the youngest. While she was impressed by his good looks and athletic physique, she wasn't sure how much disrespect she'd allow him to inflict upon her only friend.

Robby handled it well though. He was laughed nervously as he backed away from the brute. "Yeah, okay. So again, we're gonna wait about five more minutes and then um…"

"Why should we wait?" A voice behind Robby spoke up just as he was about to back into him. It was Sinus. Like, Slater, Sinus felt bold and brazen enough to remove his facemask as well.

"I agree." Former Imperial agent Brian Wells was the next to remove his mask. Everyone was immediately drawn to the warm yet confident smile he wore and the reasonable tone in which he spoke.

Brian continued. "I'm sure we're all here because we were moved by the words of the Indivisualist. I have to admit, as I read those words, something began to stir in me. And since then, I've waited every day patiently for this moment."

Priest Edwin was the next to remove his mask, catching everyone off guard with his ghostly appearance and naturally wide-eyed stare. He spoke with a raspy yet loud enunciating voice. "Anyone arriving late doesn't deserve to join us. Anyone with a burning passion or… irritation in the skin, as the Indivisualist puts it, wouldn't let anything stand in their way from coming to this fork in the road."

Others began to nod at Priest Edwin's words. Watching the bold members take off their masks and speak up made Eliza proud. "Indeed." She scoffed with a smile.

The guests all watched the hooded figure drop safely from the ledge with a smooth cat-like landing. She slowly removed her hood, releasing those long wavy golden locks. And after removing her facemask, she introduced herself.

"I'm the Indivisualist. You can call me Eliza."

There was a mild rumble amongst the guests. Everyone was stunned not only by her youth, but the fact that she was a woman with stunning looks that seemed as if she belonged in a sorority. Slater and Brian exchanged glances of disappointment, both wondering if they should feel embarrassed, ashamed or both. Oddly enough, it was only Priest Edwin and Sinus who seemed to not give a damn about Eliza's revelation. Eliza took note of the two and gave them a slight nod as to say, "Thank you for not acting like assholes."

Brian was the first to speak up, raising a hand for silence. "Eliza. Words alone won't stop the syndicate. I think most of us came here under the impression that we would organize to take action."

"Yeah! Alright! Just what the hell are we all doing here?" Slater shouted.

Eliza turned to Robby and gave him a nod. Robby understood the planned gestured and headed for the front entrance to lock the door. Several of the guests noticed Robby heading off, but were drawn to Eliza as she approached and walked amongst the midst of the group. She locked eyes with each and every one of them thoroughly. As beautiful as she was, most couldn't help but feel intimidated by her lack of concern or fear. It was as if the moment she locked eyes with them, her size suddenly grew in stature to tower over their very souls.

"Eight years ago, my father was one of the first within the Tampa Bay Police Department to theorize that the crime wave was controlled and all stemmed from a single entity. He was the first to suspect Isaac Pierce to be the head, the godfather of that syndicate. And four years ago he was butchered to death right in front of me. I was fifteen then. And Braden Pierce was his killer. I saw his face but I was told that I was too young, too traumatized to testify. There isn't any record of Braden Pierce in the system. Or that he even exists." Eliza told them.

"Then how do you know it was Braden?" Slater asked with skepticism.

"Because his name were the last words to past through my father's lips." Eliza answered.

A sullen mood swept over the members. They knew from the obvious tension in her voice that she wasn't lying. Then it suddenly hit the former SWAT captain as to who Eliza was referring to. Slater's eyes widened as he began to point. "Detective Christie? You're Detective Emil Christie's daughter?"

Eliza nodded.

"And you're the former 6th unit SWAT captain, James Slater. What of it?" Robby said much to Slater's surprise.

Robby then turned to Brian. "And you're ex-IIA, Agent Brian Wells. Most of you guys are off duty-cops or washed up former military. Big whoop."

Slater stepped up to Robby. "Hey look you little shit stain. I'm all for taking down the syndicate." He then turned to Eliza. "And I heard about your pops in the academy. He was a hero. But this isn't about settling a vendetta. This is about cleaning up our city and taking it back!"

As the other guests cheered bluntly in agreement of Slater, the former SWAT captain stepped back to get in Robby's face. Robby couldn't help but feel intimidated but held his ground. "So if you wanna join us, then you're going to have to..."

"First of all!" Eliza snapped, cutting Slater off. Eliza put more bass into her voice to give off the sound of a commander. She would later go on to use this tone in the future when out in the field.

"Everyone in this room carries a vendetta. To not recognize this is ignorance. Secondly, everyone in this room is here to join me. My team. If you leave here and make up your mind to start your own group, I'll kill you. Why? Because you'll make mistakes. Mistakes the enemy will learn from and adapt to, all of which will hinder our progress. And more importantly, it's because I'm childish like that. I admit it. I don't want the Pierce to associate me to the likes of any half-assed vigilante."

"You'll kill us huh?" Slater doubted with a grin. Eliza squared her shoulders toward the square-headed cop and gave him a long hard stare. She was almost certain that she'd have to teach him a lesson in humility in the near future.

"You call yourself an Indivisualist?" Brian asked with his arms crossed. "What about Reginald Harvey's concept on human life being the most precious thing on earth?"

Eliza scoffed as she started to walk toward the door. "Yeah well, part of being an indivisualist is the concept of making up one's own mind, to choose which philosophies to live by. The point is, to join this group means putting your lives on the line. Most of you have probably heard of the Furyx gene. Well, I'm here to tell you that it does exist and several key enforcers with the syndicate have it, namely Braden Pierce. That's why even the good cops who aren't paid up don't stand a chance against them. It's virtually suicide to take them head on."

"I kid you not, Braden is the worst of the worse and I haven't even gotten to his little brother. This isn't a club or even a team, it's a militia. And I'm your commander. Given the importance and danger of our objectives and what we're trying to accomplish, I'm making it clear here and now that any insubordination out in the field will be met with the shredding edge of my sword. Its name is Ivy. Anyone who has the slightest problem fusing with this concept…" Eliza raised her right hand and gestured toward the door.

Everyone was impressed by her declarations and some even applauded her. Priest Edwin approached her with a deadpan face, but Eliza could sense the admiration he was trying to project. "What do we call ourselves, commander?" He asked her.

With strong conviction and a nod, she answered. "We are August the 18th!"

There was a general approval with most of the members feeling the fire and passion extruding from her. They couldn't wait to begin. Even Slater's shoulders were lowered by her mysterious, yet dominating sense of entitlement. Like Robby, Slater gradually beginning to understand that she wasn't the type to be bargained with.

All Slater could ask was, "So where do we start?"

Seeing Slater's sign of submission allowed Eliza to give a sigh of relief. "From the ground up, Slater. Robby here, is my second in command. He's neither fighter nor a field agent. But he knows technology and can tell what's coming better than most psychics. He'll take it from here." Eliza instructed.

Robby clapped his hands together with a smile as most members dropped their duffle bags and gave Robby all ears. "Alright cool. Well, first thing we need to do is fortify this place and set up our security defenses."

About Stage in the Sky

Revenge, Rivalry and Rebellion, Stage in the Sky is the theater that presents the entertaining stories and essays of neo-romanticist Rock Kitaro.

When I was fifteen, I read three books that would forever change my life. The most significant was Nancy Springer's "I am Mordred." If you know your Arthurian Legend then you know that Mordred is the name of the knight who kills King Arthur. But Nancy Springer's book told the story from Mordred's point of view. It told of his upbringing, his love, his ambitions.

It was amazing. Reading her book opened my eyes to the world of perspective. Before this, and even now, it seems so many people these days forget that there are two sides or more sides to every story. Even the worst villains are heroes to somebody else. No one just rolls out of bed with a desire to cause harm. And even if they do, there's a reason. So why not let the audience decide if that reason is good enough. This is what I do with my stories.

I'll go ahead and tell you that with my stories, I curse and can sometimes be choreographic with my fight scenes. Inspired by Lord Byron, all of my main characters are troubled individuals. They are sophisticated, arrogant, seductive, disrespectful of authority, self-destructive and struggle with a sense of integrity, what's right or wrong.

Make sure to visit **www.stageinthesky.com** for Rock Kitaro's latest releases or send your regards to RockKitaro@gmail.com.

The Three Kings of Ybor Saga

Vol. 1 – Eliza Christie's Vendetta

Vol. 2 – The Wolves of the Syndicate

Vol. 3 – A Reunion of Beasts

Vol. 4 – August the 18th

Vol. 5 – The Kennedy St. Massacre

Vol. 6 – Beware of Romanticists

Vol. 7 – The Ides of March

www.ingramcontent.com/pod-product-compliance
Lightning Source LLC
Chambersburg PA
CBHW070530130626
46555CB00003B/1345